# BEACHFRONT MEMORIES

## SOLOMONS ISLAND BOOK FIVE

## MICHELE GILCREST

# GET A FREE EBOOK!

Would you like a FREE ebook? JOIN Michele's newsletter to receive information about new releases, giveaways, and special promotions! To say thank you, I'll send you a FREE copy of The Inn at Pelican Beach. Sign up today!

https://dl.bookfunnel.com/wr9wvokoin

# CHAPTER 1

*A*gnes Covington removed her apron in preparation for her shift to end. After eight long hours of serving tables, the only thing she had in mind was grabbing a latte and making a bee-line home to unwind.

She'd like to believe there would be time to work on plans for her food truck business, and maybe even a late-night meal with her sister, but exhaustion was settling in and staying up late was starting to look like a long shot.

"Pull it together, Covington," she told herself as she yawned. She then zipped up her jacket, grabbed her purse, and proceeded to leave when she bumped into her boss, Lucille.

"Lucille, I'm sorry. I didn't see you standing there. I didn't even hear you come in," she said, letting out a tired laugh.

Lucille wore her usual restaurant look with a pen wedged above her ear. "You're fine. It's my fault. I should've made more noise so I wouldn't startle you half to death."

The two paused in awkward silence. And, since Agnes didn't know what to make of it, she waited for Lucille to continue. "Agnes, I've been meaning to speak to you, but I was stuck in meetings all afternoon. I hate to bother you when you're on the way out the door, but do you have a moment?" she asked.

"Sure. It's not like I have anywhere important to be. I was just heading to the coffee shop to satisfy my nighttime addiction." She smiled.

"Ha." Lucille chuckled. "I don't know how you do it. If I drank caffeine at night, I'd be wired way into the wee hours of the morning."

"Habit, I guess. My body is used to it." Again, Agnes noticed an awkwardness about Lucille's presence, but she didn't know what to make of it. "Sooo. What's up?"

"Agnes, I don't know how to say this. My mind is blown away with the way this day is going, to be honest with you. As bizarre as it may seem, the business has taken a turn for the worst."

"I don't understand," Agnes replied.

"I can barely wrap my head around it, myself. I thought we were doing okay. But, to make things plain, the Seafood Shack is struggling financially. Our catering jobs have plummeted this year, the volume of traffic in the restaurant has been on the decline, and well... the numbers don't look too good right about now. I don't get it. We're located right on the water, and we've always been a hot spot for those who want a taste of Solomons. We should be doing better than we are."

Agnes froze, calculating the impact of what she shared. "Soooo, what you're saying is—"

"I'm trying to tell you that I hate to do it, but I have to let you go. I can't afford to pay the staff if I don't let someone go. Proper protocol would be to go with the last hired, except I have to lay off two of my employees. That would be you and Monahan." Lucille's voice dwindled down to a faint murmur. Then she continued. "I'm sorry, kiddo. You are one of my best

2

servers. Always willing to pick up the slack for others, kind to the customers, and one of the most requested by the locals. It breaks my heart to do this to you. It really does."

Agnes stared at Lucille but could barely hear her speak as she envisioned the last several months of planning for the food truck, applying for the license, making menu selections, and even stashing away start-up funds. Somehow, in this moment, all her hard work seemed to be going down the drain.

The game plan was always to keep her full-time job and start slow, working the food truck business part-time, on the side. *So much for careful planning.*

"Agnes? Are you okay?"

Lifting slowly out of a fog she replied, "Uh, yeah. You just caught me off guard. I wasn't really prepared to be unemployed. It's pretty bad timing, actually. But, then again, I guess no one can ever really be prepared at times like this. It just hits you when you least expect it," she said, swooping her fist upward, trying to make light of a not-so-light topic.

"I know, honey. Trust me when I tell you I did everything I could. The accountant and I went over the numbers forward and backward, and then one more time just to be certain. I know it may not be much, but I'm happy to give you stellar references, and the minute I figure a way out of this mess, you'll be the first person I call, just in case you want to come back." Lucille offered.

Agnes placed her hands on Lucille's shoulders. "I know you did all that you could. And, for what it's worth, I absolutely loved working for you," she said, slightly revealing her dimples. "Of course, I won't miss going home smelling like fish every day. That part you can keep. But, I'll miss everyone here. If anything changes, let me know."

"I certainly will, hun."

Agnes' hands dropped to her waist side as she walked past

Lucille. She looked down at her knee-high boots, then pushed through the swinging doors to the main dining room. Lucille was right. The traffic had lightened over the last couple of months, but she blamed it on the cold weather. Surely with March on the horizon, happy and satisfied customers would return each week. *Wouldn't they,* she thought.

She looked around one last time, waving at the remaining server on shift, and then exited the restaurant.

The drive back into the heart of Solomons Island was dreary with fog resting above the water. Technically, since she was now unemployed, the last thing she should be doing was wasting four bucks on a cup of coffee. But, it was good coffee, and she needed a place to go and think.

At forty-three, she was still living with her sister, who by the way, was about to get married. Agnes needed a plan. And she needed one fast.

Her introduction to Solomons Island wasn't exactly under the best of terms. It's not often that one moves to the island to get away from a man who was a liar and a cheat. A man who completely caused her to take a one-year sabbatical from dating. And who just so happened to be her sister's ex. But, that was beside the point.

Agnes and her sister, Clara, made amends after the tumultuous ordeal, and their rocky past was now solid and secure.

This was supposed to be her time to make a new life for herself... an independent life. And, that life was supposed to begin with the launch of her new business. Not with a pink slip and the pressure of being unemployed.

# CHAPTER 2

*G*rant Beckham gazed at the boat slowly backing up to a nearby slip. He listened as the engine shut down and watched a couple disembark, taking the necessary precautions to secure the boat for the evening.

Walking along the dock on Main Street had become a daily ritual for Grant. He liked to think of it as time for clearing his mind and perhaps providing some inspiration before starting a new chapter in his novel.

This evening he needed an extra dose of inspiration, as he suffered from a terrible case of writer's block. Something that only a long walk in nature could cure along with a healthy dose of caffeine to help him pull an all-nighter.

Grant was staying in a beach house rental, nestled along the southern tip of Solomons Island. It was his tradition to occasionally venture from home, in Tennessee, taking creative trips to spark new ideas. With views of the Patuxent and a beautiful sunrise each morning, this trip would be no exception.

He watched as the couple passed by, walking hand in hand, and offered a brief smile while buttoning his jacket, covering himself from the chilly March breeze. Once the atmosphere was clear he returned to listening to the sound of the water. Unfortunately, the only thing that came to him was growing frustration, as he wasn't any closer to having a new idea for his book than he was when he first began his walk.

He tugged on the collar of his jacket and buried his hands in his pockets. With one last glance toward the water, Grant turned and quickly found himself submerged in hot beverage with foam, crashing head on into a woman he'd encountered several times since he'd arrived at the island. He overheard others refer to her as Agnes, but in his mind, he secretly named her Safire. She was an attractive red head, with a fiery personality. And, now he was covered in her coffee. Not at all what he had in mind for a spark of creativity and a peaceful evening.

"Good grief," he called out, startled at the exchange.

She jumped back, examining the cup on the ground and then his jacket, which was now covered in milky brown liquid, but she didn't say a word.

So, instead Grant broke the silence. "No worries. I'm fine. Just a little wet, but thankfully my coat protected me from potential third-degree burns. No need to check on me or anything," he said, sarcastically, still dangling his arms in the air.

"I'm sorry," she said, letting out a breath. "Not trying to be mean or anything, but you wouldn't be covered in latte if you were watching where you were going," Agnes replied.

"Seriously? Are you really blaming me when you were the one walking toward me and—"

"And what?" she asked.

"You know what. Forget it."

"No, go ahead. Say it."

Mentally, he hit the reset button, deciding it would be best to start over.

6

"It doesn't matter how it happened. It was an accident. Neither of us meant anything by it." He offered, trying to be diplomatic about the situation. But before he could continue, he noticed she was getting a little choked up.

*What in the world?* he thought to himself.

"It was just a little spill... these things happen. Please, don't get upset. I'll just run into the coffee shop and grab a few napkins. This isn't anything the cleaners can't fix," he said, reaching out to console her as best as he could.

"No," she muttered.

"No?"

"It's not that. I mean— I'm sorry. I'm just having a really bad day. I worked a long shift and was then politely laid off by my boss. I thought I'd come here just to clear my head before going home and now—"

She pointed toward his jacket and then picked the cup off the ground. "It was probably my fault. For all I know I was just lost in a daze, not paying attention to where I was going."

"Hey, again. Don't worry about it."

She inspected his jacket. "The least I can do is walk back to the coffee shop with you and ask Harvey to grab some towels for us. Real towels instead of those flimsy napkins that will disintegrate all over the material," she said, and then motioned for him to follow her across the street.

"You really don't have to do this. I'm perfectly fine," he said.

"I know I don't, but as I said earlier, it's the least I can do. So, come on, let's go. We could be inside drying off by now." She waved her hand for him to step down off the curb, but he didn't move, still processing the moment.

"Are you always this —" She stopped herself.

"This what?"

"I don't know. Stubborn? Maybe even a tad annoying?" She murmured under her breath with a smile.

"Hold on a second. Stubborn I can accept, but annoying? You barely know me. And anytime we do see each other, you're normally in a rush. Hence the whole latte episode," he said, pointing to his jacket.

"Okay, that was low," she replied, then marched toward the coffee shop without him.

Grant watched her walk off, then looked down, shaking his head at the sight of his jacket.

*Well, here goes nothing.* He followed Agnes into the coffee shop.

Inside, she was standing toward the back, receiving a white towel from Harvey, the cashier. He revealed a look of surprise when he saw Grant laced with fresh latte stains.

"Yikes, looks like you might need a second towel." Harvey offered.

"Hey, Harvey, I think I'm okay. One towel is fine."

Agnes ignored him and proceeded to dab his jacket, methodically soaking up the moisture while leaving Grant speechless. Was she really attending to his clothing after calling him annoying and walking away? That's what he wanted to ask, but all he could manage to do was breathe in her scent and hope that his heart would stop palpitating loud enough for her to hear.

"Harvey, would you mind wetting this end of the towel with water?" she asked.

Grant gazed at her red locks and her curvature as she leaned over the counter. The way she flipped her hair back increased the tempo of his pulse, but he had to snap out of it, remembering the reason he was there in the first place.

"Harvey, I'm good. You don't have to do that. I'm staying just a short hop up the road and can take care of this in no time," he said.

But, apparently, his words held no merit as Agnes gave Harvey a nod, pleading for him to dampen the towel just the same.

"You have a hard time taking no for an answer I see." Grant smiled.

"You followed me over here, and you're still standing here waiting for help. That's not exactly a refusal, if you ask me."

"Touché," he replied, wondering why such a beautiful woman always appeared to be rough around the edges. Then again, maybe he just brought out this side of her personality. Everyone else he'd ever observed her talking to always appeared to have a pleasant exchange filled with smiles and laughter. Maybe it was just their chemistry.

"Thanks, Harvey. Now. Where were we?" She kneaded the wet end of the towel into his jacket in circular motions, applying the necessary pressure to lift the stain.

A part of him felt a little silly, standing there while she tended to his clothing. Harvey, on the other hand, seemed to be entertained by it all, while the few customers lingering around the shop ignored them all together.

"The stain is lifting a little bit, but you definitely should throw this bad boy in the wash when you get home," she said.

"Eh, I'll just drop it off at the dry cleaners."

"What's the matter? Afraid to get your hands dirty?" she asked.

"No, I just have a deadline to meet and not a lot of time to fuss over a jacket. I'm sure I can pick up a new one in the morning or have one sent overnight."

Agnes dabbed the towel one last time, then took a step back.

"There. That should hold you over until you decide what you want to do. If it were me, I'd wash it at home and save a few bucks. But, if you insist on taking it to the cleaners, then please — let me pay for it. It's the only way I can walk away with a clear conscience."

"Ah, so she does have a warm side to her after all." He laughed.

"What's that supposed to mean?"

"I tried to strike up a little small talk with you during the holidays, and you hightailed it out of here so fast one would've thought I had a disease. We were still in the middle of a conversation for goodness' sake. You probably wouldn't be talking to me now if you hadn't dowsed me in hot coffee." He teased.

Agnes looked over at Harvey, who excused himself. She then looked Grant in the eyes.

"Look, it's no fault of your own, but I'm having a rough day. I'm sorry, I couldn't get the stain out completely, but I'm offering to pay your cleaner's bill. Are you going to take me up on the offer or not?" she asked, sounding very matter of fact.

"I'd like to counter-offer your offer."

"What?"

"I said, I'd like to counter your offer. Forget the jacket. Instead, sit down and have coffee with me and unload about your day."

He knew it was a leap. Probably one he shouldn't be taking with such a fiery personality and with his pending deadline. But, he was intrigued by her, and you could say, his curiosity was getting the best of him.

"Are you nuts?" she asked.

"Probably." He chuckled. "No. Seriously. I selfishly need a

break from my writer's block, and you clearly need to unleash the frustrations of the day. If you're offering to do something for me, then I'm asking you... nicely... to stay and have coffee with me."

Grant held his breath, again hoping that she couldn't hear his heart beating out of his chest. This time his nerves were anticipating a solid no. But it wasn't going to kill him to at least try. *What's the worst that could happen?*

He'd been on the island longer than expected, and outside of the occasional conversations with some of the locals and Harvey, he'd pretty much been alone.

Agnes looked at her watch, which prompted him to prod her a little bit more. "You might as well. The whole point of you coming here was to get a cup of coffee, wasn't it?"

"Yes, by myself, of course."

"Come onnn. I'm harmless. Even Harvey can vouch for that, right, Harvey?" Grant gestured.

"Yes, sir. It's been a pleasure having Mr. Beckham around," he replied with a wink.

Both men waited for a response from Agnes.

"Okay, one coffee, and then I have to go," she said.

Grant smiled, revealing his dimples. "Harvey, can we have a second round of whatever beverage I'm wearing on my jacket... make that two orders. I might as well have a taste for myself."

"Ha ha, Mr. Funny Guy. The jokes just keep coming. I really think you should let me make this right so I don't have to be tormented from now until the end of time," she said.

"Hmm, the thought of knowing you that long does sound enticing, but sadly, I'm leaving in a couple of weeks, maybe a month, tops."

The entire time he spoke he never took his eyes off Agnes. He even managed to reach into his pocket and slip a twenty-dollar bill on the counter without breaking his gaze into her eyes.

"That's right, word around the island is you're here writing a novel. What do you write, again? Mysteries? Thrillers?" she asked.

"Not quite. Do I look like a thriller kind of guy to you?"

"Well, you were standing by the dock wearing a camel peacoat fit for a detective who's trying to solve a crime. It was just a guess, but a pretty darn good one, I'd say, based on your appearance."

Grant chuckled a little, finding it difficult to figure her out. It wasn't always what she said, but how she said it, that captured his attention. For the first time, he was discovering his newfound attraction for someone with a touch of sass.

"Is it a secret?" she asked.

"Not necessarily. I just like to keep a low profile, working as a traveling writer. Living life under the radar kind of suits my personality. I'm not one for the limelight."

"Yeah, but if this is your full-time career, I'm sure people know who you are. Anybody can find Grant Beckham on the internet, right?"

"Perhaps, but you won't come up with much, other than my address in Tennessee. I write under a pen name," he said.

Grant reached for the coffee cups that Harvey left on the counter and handed one to Agnes.

"Shall we?" he said, extending his hand so they could take a walk.

"I thought we were going to stay here."

"And have you be seen sitting with the detective slash author guy from out of town? People may talk. A walk along the dock might be a safer bet." He teased.

"The jokes just keep coming with you. If I didn't know any better, I'd think you were a standup comedian."

Grant waved, thanking Harvey and gesturing for him to keep the change. He then held the door open for Agnes, catching the fresh scent of her hair as she walked by.

Before she was able to get too far ahead, he stopped her. "I'd like to call a truce and perhaps start over. All the joking around is just lighthearted fun on my part, but I'll stop if it bothers you. Besides, I'd much rather pick up where we left off the last time I saw you. You know, the point in the conversation where you were telling me about living with your sister and starting your own business."

She looked surprised.

"You remember that?" she asked.

He finished taking a sip of his coffee. "Well, yes, of course. It's not every day that I come across a beautiful woman with strawberry red hair who divulges her life story to me in a coffee shop."

A warm smile washed over her face. Even if it was only momentary, he saw it, but decided to tuck it away in his memory bank with every other encounter they'd had.

Agnes relaxed her shoulders. "Clearly, the people out here are having an effect on me."

"That's not a bad thing. I love how warm and welcoming everyone is on the island. It's one of the reasons I decided to extend my trip, along with the delicious seafood and gorgeous nautical views. This place has been a great source of inspiration for my writing," he responded.

Grant invited her to walk across the street to finish their coffee by the dock. Somehow, he'd completely forgotten about being chilly earlier or that he was still technically wearing stained attire.

"How's that working out for you? The novel that is—" she asked.

"It was going great all the way up until seven o'clock this

morning when I hit a brick wall. I think most refer to it as writer's block. But, nothing I can't push through."

For some odd reason Grant felt like he could talk to her all night, sharing his life story and listening to hers. Of course, he knew it wasn't realistic, but a man could dream.

"Enough about me, you're the one who had a rough day and need to unload. Whatever you divulge, know that your secret is totally safe with me. No judgement, no questions asked."

He tilted his head, waiting for her to respond or crack a smile or do something. And when she finally did laugh, all he could do was study her dimples, trying not to be too obvious while he did it.

"First of all, it didn't go unnoticed that you still haven't told me what you write," she said, placing her hand on her hip.

"Touché, touché. How about we make a deal? You tell me about your day, since it's the reason why we grabbed coffee... well, at least part of the reason, and then, if you promise to keep it between us, I'll share my genre."

She took another sip from her cup.

"Deal," Agnes said, clearing her throat. "My story is rather simple. As I mentioned to you a while back, I live here in Solomons with my sister, Clara. She works over at Lighthouse Tours, with her fiancé, Mike."

"Sure, I've heard of them. They're the ones who ran the Christmas Nights fundraiser back in December," he said.

"That's them."

She nodded. "I left my home state of New York and moved in with her temporarily until I can get on my feet. The game plan was to hold on to my full-time job waiting tables and stash away the necessary funds, so that I could start a part-time food truck on the side. Over time, if the business grew, I was going to reevaluate the gig at the restaurant, but until then —"

She drew in a breath. "Until then, I had already applied for the proper licensing, purchased the truck, and jumped through all the necessary hoops. Now that I don't have a job, I can no longer afford to focus my attention on the truck. So, there goes that idea. Poof, just like that."

"I'm sorry. Did your boss explain why she was laying you off?"

"Yeah, she said they don't have enough money to keep myself and one other on board. With the slowdown in customers, I probably should've seen it coming."

While she spoke, Grant noticed her forearm was inches from his as they both leaned on the banister overlooking the water. Being that close to her felt good.

"Maybe this is just the push you need to go full time with the food truck. Perhaps the job would've held you back," he said.

"No bueno."

"Ah, she speaks Spanish, I see." He smiled.

"Not really. I just picked up a word or two from the kids on the old block where I grew up. I can't carry a conversation in Spanish to save my life."

"Well, you could've fooled me. You even said it with an accent. I nearly—"

"Grant," she said, cutting him off mid-sentence.

"Yes." He felt an electrical current, which intensified when she called his name. He just hoped the attraction wasn't one-sided. No sooner had he thought it, than her demeanor changed.

"Let's cut to the chase. What are we doing? Standing here, drinking coffee, and making small talk about my problems? This won't make the stain on your jacket disappear any faster, and it's certainly not going to lead to anything." She grumbled.

"Whoa, whoa. Wait a minute. Am I such a bad guy for

trying to be nice to you? For being a gentleman? How do you know what it will or will not lead to? Every time we run into each other you look at me with the same level of intrigue as I do with you."

"Well, aren't you confident?" she said.

"Come on. You know what I mean."

"No. I don't. I never expressed to you that I'm intrigued by anything."

"Interesting." He huffed.

Agnes faced the water and let out a deep-throated sound of aggravation. "See, this is exactly how it starts with men. They smile, show off their cute dimples, they always say the right things, and then before you know it, bam, I'm in trouble. I'm not doing it this time. Nope. Not doing it," she said, arguing with herself.

"Who are you talking to?" Before Grant could gather his thoughts, Agnes placed her coffee on the railing, grabbed him by the jacket, and planted a warm, sensual kiss on the lips. When she stopped, he was still all puckered up, yearning for more, until he slowly opened his eyes, realizing it was over.

She adjusted her breathing, looking almost surprised, like she enjoyed it, but he couldn't quite tell.

"There. Now that we've satisfied our curiosity or intrigue as you would say, I can return to my sabbatical, and you can return to your author life."

He watched as she shifted her handbag and grabbed her cup of coffee.

*Sabbatical?* he thought.

"Have a good evening. Again, sorry about the jacket," she said.

The same way she appeared out of nowhere, she left, disappearing into the darkness of the night, leaving Grant speechless.

# CHAPTER 3

$\mathcal{C}$ lara Covington skimmed through her emails while sinking her teeth into a warm glazed donut. She'd consciously made a decision to cut the donut in half, knowing the extra calories might mess with her upcoming wedding dress alterations, a decision she couldn't afford to make. Although some suggested she might want to wait another month or so, she knew with monitoring her diet and keeping a strict exercise regiment, she would be fine. At least she hoped.

To the left of her computer was a stack of mail for Lighthouse Tours, and to her right, a list of clients that needed to be confirmed for this week's boat tours. But for the moment, all she could manage to do was breeze through emails and daydream over a picture of her and Mike. He was the man who still gave her goosebumps anytime he snuck up to embrace her from behind, and the man she'd soon call husband.

The sound of bells ringing at the entrance of the store soon broke her train of thought.

"Agnes? What are you doing here?" she asked.

"Good morning to you, too, sis. Nice to see you. Would I like a cup of coffee? Sure, I'd love to have one," Agnes responded.

Clara crumpled up a piece of paper and tossed it at her head.

"That's not what I meant. I'm just surprised to see you here, with your sassy mouth." Clara smiled.

"I know, and I apologize for not calling first, but you were already upstairs when I got in last night and I really need to talk to you."

Just then, the bells rang again and in came Ms. Mae, followed by her husband, Jonathan, and their co-worker Tommy, all who were scheduled to run a tour at some point throughout the day.

"This is rare. All three of you coming in at the same time. Surely you must've carpooled with one another," Clara said.

"No, we ran into Tommy on the way coming in, that's all." Ms. Mae stopped at the front counter to admire Agnes. "How are you, darlin? It's been a while."

"I've seen better days, Ms. Mae, but I'm hanging in there. Hi, Jonathan...hey, Tommy." She waved.

"Good to see you, Agnes." Jonathan and Tommy greeted her and then left the women to speak among themselves.

Clara leaned in. "You've seen better days? What's going on with you?"

"Well." She winced then proceeded to nervously clear her throat. "That's why I stopped by."

Sensing hesitation from Agnes, Clara shifted the conversation to Ms. Mae.

"Mike should be back in about an hour. He's down at the warehouse preparing a few boats for the owners. He mentioned something about your boat... I think he wanted to see if you guys were ready to crank her up or if you wanted to wait another month."

"Thank you, Clara. I'll say something to Jonathan and let him handle it. In the meantime, Agnes, it's so good to see you. Don't be a stranger. We'd love to see you around more often," Ms. Mae said, smiling.

"Oh, I'll be around, all right." Agnes mumbled under her breath, but it was loud enough to catch Clara's attention.

Once the room was free of interruptions, Clara folded her arms, positioning herself to listen. "Spill it."

"Why do you have to say it like that? It's not like I did anything wrong. Well. Technically, I may have committed one bizarre act that was completely out of character, but I blame that on the emotional exhaustion from the day's events." Agnes rambled.

"Agnes," Clara said, slightly raising her voice.

"What?"

"You don't usually show up at my job or call my job unless there's a problem. So, what's wrong? Spill it. You're making me nervous, already."

"Trust me, I'm the one who needs to be nervous, not you. I don't know any better way to say this than to just come out with it. I'm officially unemployed. Lucille gave me a pink slip yesterday. Technically, she laid two of us off. Myself and Monahan. She said the finances weren't looking good and she had to follow proper protocol, letting go of the last hired. But, since she needed to let go of two people, I was next on the list."

"Oh, no. I'm sorry, Ag."

Clara recognized the familiar sound of swallowing, something Agnes did whenever she was trying to fight back tears.

"All the hard work and planning for the food truck. All of it, down the drain in a matter of seconds. Poof. Just like that, I have to put everything on hold," she said.

"Do you? You have everything from the menu, the food supplier, the truck. What else do you need?"

"I can't run this part-time startup without a steady full-time job to provide capital on the back end. It's the only way to do this where I can sleep at night, knowing I'm not minutes way from going into debt."

"Hmm. Most of my funds are locked away in various investment accounts, but I'm happy to help in whatever way I can."

"Clara, you've already done enough. If it weren't for you, I wouldn't have the truck. I always appreciate how supportive you are, but I need to do this the right way, starting at square one, which is getting a new job."

She watched as Agnes paced over to the front window, watching pedestrians as they passed by.

"Anyway, I just wanted to tell you right away, and reassure you that I'll get on the interview trail immediately. I'm sure you and Mike want to begin your lives as Mr. and Mrs. living in your house alone," she said.

"Is that what you're worried about? Agnes, the basement apartment is yours for as long as you need it. That's something both Mike and I strongly agree on. We're not even getting married until the summer, but even if it were tomorrow, please have peace of mind in knowing that house is big enough for all three of us, plus the dog."

Agnes chuckled in amusement at the thought of Holly running around.

"Don't worry, Ag. We'll help you figure something out."

"Thank you. Oh, and by the way. There's one other thing you should know before you hear it from some passerby on the island," Agnes said.

"If it has anything to do with this bizarre act which was completely out of character, please, do tell."

"That's exactly what it's about," Agnes replied, inching toward the front door and placing her hand on the handle. "You know that author who's been smiling at me for a while?" she asked.

"Yeah, the cute guy who's renting a beach house. I still can't believe after all this time nobody knows what he writes."

"Me either. But I know this much. He's a pretty darn good kisser."

"What?" Clara leapt up from behind her desk, watching as Agnes slipped out of the door, waving back at her through the glass window.

"I'm going to search for a new job. We'll talk more when you get home," she yelled through the window, and then left.

*Oh, Agnes,* Clara thought to herself.

"Jonathan, I have a bone to pick with you," Mae, said, while unpacking brochures in the break area.

Mae Middleton knew she wouldn't make it through the day without finishing the conversation she'd started with her husband on the drive into work. For the most part she tried not to bring up personal matters at Lighthouse Tours, but her flesh was having a hard time letting the topic go.

Their work at the shop giving boat tours kept them busy, giving them something to do while building up a second retirement nest egg. But sometimes being married and working full time together had its benefits, and other times not so much.

"Mae, we're not having this conversation while we're on the clock. Besides, it's utterly ridiculous, and I don't understand why you keep bringing it up." Jonathan murmured.

She watched as he scanned the key rack for the keys to his boat.

"A woman knows when her husband is distracted, perhaps even a bit inattentive," she said, lowering her voice. Then she continued. "And a woman also knows when there's someone trying to vie for her husband's attention. The new neighbor, Edith, who moved into the Zimmerman's old house has been nothing but a nuisance since the day she stepped foot on the island. *Jonathan, can you help me with my garage opener? Jonathan, can you fix my mailbox for me?*" Mae said, imitating Edith's voice. "We have chores of our own that need tending to. The honey-do list is growing by the hour," she said.

Jonathan stopped what he was doing and turned around, smiling at Mae.

"Anna Mae, it's not my fault. She approached me, not the other way around." His smile broadened. "Do I detect a little jealousy?" Jonathan asked.

Feeling her blood boiling inside, Mae let the next stack of brochures slap down on the table.

"I'm not jealous, Jonathan. But, I know how to fix the problem if you won't. Perhaps she needs to hear from me direct- ly," Mae replied.

"You wouldn't."

"I would. I'll be cordial. I'll even bake up a batch of fresh cookies and hand deliver them, along with a clear message that my husband is not the neighborhood handyman," she replied, pouting as she returned to her busy work.

"Mae, that's not like you. You're always warm and welcoming to the neighbors. Everyone except for Meredith next door, however. She's always been an exception to the rule."

"Yes, and even then, we still managed to have her over for the holidays so she wouldn't be alone. This is different. Edith is practically a stranger, yet all too comfortable with you. It's time to put an end to it." She grumbled.

"Aww, Mae."

Just then Mike popped his head in, wishing them a good morning.

"I thought I heard you two back here. Everything okay?" he asked.

"Everything is fine. Nothing a second cup of coffee can't cure," Jonathan responded, looking over at Mae.

Mae forced herself to put on a smile, even though she knew the matter was hardly over.

"Good to see you, Mike."

"Likewise, Ms. Mae. I just checked the forecast, and it looks like it's going to be a beautiful day for giving tours."

"I'm looking forward to it. I could use the fresh air."

She sensed that Mike was curious and may have heard a portion of their conversation. Thankfully, they'd all worked together long enough that she knew he'd let it go and wouldn't probe.

"Alrighty. Well, I'm sure you two need time to get ready for the day, and I need to check in with Clara on a few things. Break a leg out there today." He chuckled, then left them to their conversation.

Clara cracked open the blinds in Mike's office and planted herself across from his desk with her legal pad and pen in hand. It was their ritual whenever he wasn't working at the North Beach office to begin the week reviewing the upcoming tours, marketing, and staff assignments. Today, she had one other pressing matter on her mind.

She stood, giving him a good morning kiss when he entered the room, before taking her seat again.

"Hey, babe," she said, releasing a sigh.

"Uh, oh. That doesn't sound good. Talk to me. What's on your mind?"

"Nothing that can't be resolved. Agnes stopped by this morning," she replied.

"Everything all right?"

"No. She lost her job. She said the restaurant was struggling and they needed to let her go."

"That stinks, I'm sorry to hear it." Mike leaned back in his chair with a concerned expression across his brow.

"Tell me about it. I think she's most concerned about the food truck. Working at the Seafood Shack was supposed to be a stepping stone to help her get the truck up and running," Clara responded.

"Is there anything we can do to help her?" he asked.

"I've been thinking about it ever since she left. I tried to reassure her that she has a place to stay for as long as she needs it. But I was thinking. I know you mentioned something about needing extra help at the warehouse. Having Brody there over the last month has been great, but he has to get back to having the flexibility of working between Solomons and North Beach. After all, we need him overseeing the mechanical logistics, not the warehouse, wouldn't you agree?" Clara asked.

"Agreed, and I think I see where you're going with this. Maybe it would be a good fit for her to work side by side with the new guy, Ben. We need him for the physical aspect of the job, but if she's willing, it might be nice to have a trusted family member over there as well."

"Really?" Clara asked, sounding upbeat.

"Yeah, I don't see why not. Of course, your sister is the one who needs to be excited about it, not us. Do you think she'd really be interested in checking in customers as they arrive and keeping up with the clerical aspect of the warehouse?"

"I'll ask her to be certain, but the last time I checked, it's better than being jobless. She'd be a part of the family business while still maintaining her goals with the food truck. Sounds like a win win to me," Clara said.

"Well, all right. Talk to her and then get back to me. I'm anxious to hear how she responds."

"Will do. Now, onto the next important item on the agenda," Clara said.

"You and me eloping?"

Her legal pad slid down to the floor.

"What?"

Mike sat with his back stiff as a board. "I know, not exactly what you were expecting this morning, but hear me out. Picture you and me on a flight heading to our ten-day honeymoon, by the first of the month, instead of late summer. We can go snorkeling, horseback riding along the beach, romantic dinners for two, and exchange our vows while we're there," he said, reaching his hand across the desk.

"Mike, stop it." She giggled. "You have to be kidding me, right?"

"No. I'm very serious. It may sound a little off the cuff, but I'm thrilled at the thought of stealing away with you and getting married early. We've waited long enough, and if the truth be told, we need the time away, now. I don't know about you, but I'm exhausted and can't think of anything better to do than spend two weeks away with my wife."

"But, what about your parents, my sister, and our closest friends? They all have their hearts set on seeing us get married this summer," she replied.

Mike tapped his fingers on his desk, thinking feverishly.

"Then, let's rework our plans. Let's celebrate with everybody this summer. My parents will support us no matter what, and you know folks like Jonathan and Mae understand. They eloped themselves, remember?" he asked.

Clara hesitated. "You seriously want to do this?"

"Why not? I'm ready to live my best life with you. I'm sorry, our best lives with each other." He clarified.

Her eyes shifted away as she thought of the last wishes of her former boss, Joan, before her passing.

*You have your whole life ahead of you. Live it to the fullest. I don't want you to have regrets and end up old like me, without experiencing the kind of passion and fire that comes with falling in love. You've served everyone well in your life, but it's time to think about yourself, dear. Get out there. Open up your heart and make yourself available to love. Promise me you will."*

"Clara," he called out.

She shook her head out of the daze.

"Let's do it. Let's get married next month in Hawaii. Just the two of us."

"Really?" he asked.

"Why not? I actually think it's a very romantic idea. Of course, we may want to hold off on getting our hopes up. The hotel and airlines may not be in favor of our plans," she said.

"I can work a little magic with my sky miles. It's the hotel that I'm nervous about."

Clara leaned over the desk, stopping within inches of Mike's nose. She was close enough to feel the warmth of his breath. She watched him close his eye lids, breathing in the scent of her perfume as he often did whenever she was near.

"Mike Sanders," she whispered.

"Yes,"

"I love you." She continued to whisper, then drew in his bottom lip, meeting his expectation of a kiss.

The kiss lasted for what felt like seconds before they were startled by Ms. Mae bursting in the door.

"The café is on fire. Everyone is gathered out in the street," she yelled.

The pure shock of what she said left Clara dumbfounded, fumbling on her way outside to check on the owner and her dear friend, Mackenzie.

# CHAPTER 4

*M*ackenzie watched the firefighters from engine thirty-two hose down the back of her roof, along with the entire brick and mortar next door. Tears streamed down her eyes as she stood, arms locked, with the owner of the nickel and dime store, her neighbor, and the one responsible for the fire.

"It's going to be okay, Beth. See, the firefighters have everything under control," Mack said, not knowing if that was really the case.

Apparently, one of Beth's employees had left something burning on a hot plate next door. Mack could clearly see the entire café was standing strong, but the amount of damage coming from the shared wall between them was still left to be seen.

Mackenzie's staff stood nearby with several customers, watching the scene unfold when Clara and Mike ran over.

"Clara..." she barely whispered, trying to hold back her emotions.

"Mackenzie, there you are. Are you okay?" Clara asked.

"We're fine. It was just a little accident with a hot plate. I tried to reassure Beth that the firefighters have everything under control."

Mack talked a good game, but she had a lot riding on the building in front of her with burn marks near the edge of the rooftop. At the beginning of the new year, she'd taken on a lease-to-own contract, with dreams of making a good living for herself and her daughter, Stephanie. Now, those dreams were sinking to the pit of her stomach as she wondered what the outcome of the fire would be.

"Thank you for coming over, love. If I'm not mistaken, I think Agnes is here among the crowd. Or at least she was here working on her laptop right before the fire alarm went off," Mackenzie said, peering around and spotting Agnes.

She waved her hand. "I'm right here. Just checking on some of the seniors who were sitting in the back when the alarm went off. Everyone seems to be okay. How are you doing?" Agnes asked.

Mack kindly checked in with Beth, reassuring her that everything would be okay before stepping away to talk to the Covington sisters.

"I'm nervous. I need you to send up a prayer for me, ladies, I really do. I have everything riding on this business, and I can't afford to stand here and watch it go up in flames." Mackenzie wept for a moment, then dabbed her eyes.

"If it wasn't for Chef Harold noticing the smoke coming through a vent, I don't know what we would've done." She continued.

Mike spoke up, consoling her as best as he knew how.

"I'm going to tell you the same thing you just told Beth. The firefighters have everything under control and it's all going to be fine."

"Thank you, Mike." She acknowledged.

Brody, Mack's boyfriend, was the last to appear through the crowd, giving her a bear hug just in time before the next round of tears began falling.

"I'm sorry, I got here as soon as I heard the news," he said.

"Word travels pretty fast," she responded.

"Not fast enough. Looks like the whole team is out here. The real question is, how are you holding up?"

"Physically, I'm fine. We're all fine. Thankfully, everyone was able to make it out with no injuries. The fire started over at Betty's. The poor thing. She's just as frazzled as I am. Brody, the timing couldn't be worse. Not that there's ever a good time for a fire, but I just signed the contract. I mean... I'm thankful the building is still standing, but what if the damage is bad enough to put us out of business for a while? I have a little girl to think about," she said, frantically.

"Mackenzie. Breathe."

"I can't." She wept.

"Come on. I know you can. I know this is not easy, but you are going to get through it. You're going to come out stronger on the other side. Trust me on this. Repeat after me... What's the worst thing that could happen?"

"What's the worst thing that could happen?" she said, not sounding nearly as confident as Brody.

He chuckled.

"Now, try to answer that question. What's the worst that could happen if you really take the time to think about it?"

"I don't know. I might have to hurry and find a new job before next month's rent is due. The idea of getting behind on my personal bills and the lease for the café sounds pretty stressful, if you ask me."

"Mackenzie, the worst that could happen is the insurance will cover the damage. And since you're not technically the sole owner until you're done paying off your end of the agreement, hopefully the seller will work with you. And finally, you know how much I love you and Stephanie, right?"

She nodded.

"Good. Then you should know I would never allow the two of you to stress about paying the bills. I'd help you pack your things and come live with me first. There's plenty of space for you guys. So, please. Dry your eyes. I'm here for you. We're all here for you. Everything will work out just fine," he responded.

Mack glanced over at the building and then surveyed the area. Her customers from the bridge club were gathered, retelling their versions of what happened, and her friends from Lighthouse Tours were there, showing their support. Brody was right. It was a little nerve-wracking, but this truly wasn't the end of the world.

She wiped her face and smiled a little. "Brody, what would I do without you?"

"You'd continue being the strong woman you are, figuring the whole thing out as you always do."

"Thank you. But, obviously, I still needed the pep talk. You always know the right thing to say," she replied as they turned to face the firefighters walking straight toward them.

Agnes Covington waited for the crowd to thin out before talking one-on-one with Clara. "Man, I feel bad for Mack. I'm sure she had way better plans for the start of her day."

"Tell me about it. For me, it's a cautious reminder of how important it is to focus on one thing at a time. It's way too easy to forget about things like the coffee pot or the toaster oven whenever I'm busy at work."

"True."

They continued watching Mack talk to the officials with

their arms folded. Neither of them said a word for a moment before Agnes broke the silence.

"So, I suppose you want to know about the kiss?" She offered, staring straight ahead.

"Yes, now that you mention it. I was wondering how you managed to go from unemployed to kissing a complete stranger all in the same day."

Agnes could feel Clara gazing at her, but she continued to look forward.

"He's not a complete stranger. He's a familiar stranger. One that seems to show up almost at every corner I turn," she replied.

"Again, what does this have to do with kissing him?"

"Nothing, really. Other than he caught me at an odd moment," she said.

"What odd moment?"

"Mmm. Call it a moment of weakness, if you will. Have you ever found yourself in a place where you're not looking for something, but because you're not looking for it — it's actually everywhere? I mean...technically this thing annoys the heck out of you, and you really don't want to have anything to do with it. But, you still find yourself a little curious about it. So, you finally do something to satisfy your curiosity, but then regret it the moment you do it, realizing it was just coming from a place of misplaced emotions." She paused, working hard to catch her breath.

"Agnes, what the heck are you talking about?" Clara growled.

"Hang in there. I'm getting to the point." She paced around until finally meeting Clara face to face. "Call it a moment of weakness. Perhaps even the old Agnes rearing her ugly head. But I was in a mood. I had just left from having the conversation with Lucille and was feeling pretty low. I could see all my hard work prepping for the food truck going down the tubes and it put me in a bad space. Then I ran into him." Agnes explained.

"The author?"

"Yes. The somewhat annoying, yet hot, and even a little flirtatious, writer. Now, I'll admit, since I've been refraining from dating, I've been pretty good. I've stayed laser focused and on a mission to make something of myself out here. But it's not easy, Clara. I live with my successful sister whose life is perfect in every way—"

"Hey, leave me out of this," Clara said, pointing her finger.

"All right. No excuses. But, to finish the story, I accidentally spilled coffee on the guy, and as a favor in return, when he asked me to join him for a cup of coffee —"

"You kissed him?"

Agnes laughed. "It didn't happen exactly like that. I felt a vibe between us. I can tell that he's into me a little," she said, pinching her thumb and her index finger together.

"Mm hmm. What makes you so sure?"

Agnes continued. "You were the one who pointed this out back during Christmas Nights. Plus, he's always trying to make small talk, sometimes to the point of being annoying. And finally, I literally doused the guy in my latte, and he still asked me to have coffee with him. So, I did."

"And then you kissed him?" Clara asked.

"Yep. Call it a moment of temporary insanity. But, if it makes you feel any better, I told him I was returning to my sabbatical. That should totally squash any future interest, and before you know it, he'll leave as soon as he finishes his book."

Agnes noticed Clara frowning, as if deep in thought.

"Are you certain the same woman gave birth to us?" she replied with a huge smirk smeared across her face.

"Yes, although sometimes I wonder, Miss Perfect." Agnes teased.

Laughter broke out between them.

"I'll go on record that you're probably interested in the author more than you care to admit. And, at this point, your sabbatical is rather obsolete. But that's your call, not mine."

"Trust me when I tell you. The sabbatical is back on. I arrived here several months ago fresh off of having trouble with men. I'm not going there anymore, Clara. I need to stay focused."

Clara rolled her eyes. "Whatever you say. Look, in the meantime, I have news for you. Something that I want you to think long and hard about before you respond."

"Okay."

"Mike wants to offer you a position at the warehouse, if you're interested. I told him about the layoff, and he thought it might be nice to have a family member working with the new guy, overseeing the clerical tasks, and helping out with the customers at the warehouse."

Agnes wanted to squeal at the top of her lungs, feeling so relieved at the idea. "Is it a full-time position? As in, enough hours for me to continue with my plans for the business?"

"Yes. I would imagine the salary would be comparable to what you were making at the restaurant, if not better. Plus, if you seek out the right location, you could set up your food truck here on the island instead of working further north like you originally planned."

"Clara!" she said in a high-pitched tone.

"Hang on, now. I really want you to give this serious thought. Yes, Mike needs the help and you need a job, but, is this what you really want to do? I'd hate to see you commit and then change your mind later."

"Clara, about an hour ago I was looking at becoming a

professional dog walker. I love animals, don't get me wrong, but I think customer service is more in line with my skill set, don't you?"

"Okay, just making sure." Clara looked around, presumably checking for Mack and skimming the crowd. Then she continued. "I'll tell you what. Take another day to think it over. Just to be sure. If I were you, I'd even go spend a couple of hours at the coffee shop browsing through the want ads one last time, just to be certain there's nothing else that catches your eye. If you still feel this way about the job tomorrow, then it's yours. Deal?"

"Deal. Thank you so much for this, Clara. I promise you won't regret it."

"That's what sisters are for. Now, go on. Get out of here. You have some research to do." Clara urged.

"Okay, please tell Mack that I'm willing to offer a helping hand if she needs it."

"Will do. Oh, and Agnes, one more thing before you go."

"Sure, what's up?"

"I have a bit of a bombshell to drop on you, somewhat similar to the way you dropped one on me this morning."

"You kissed another man, too?" Agnes chuckled.

"Nooo, of course not. You know that Mike's the only guy for me. But, we do plan on kissing under the stars next month as Mr. and Mrs. Sanders."

"What do you mean?"

"We're ditching the wedding plans and eloping," Clara said.

"Shut up! You? Clara Covington?"

"The one and only. I know how to live life on the edge every once in a while, you know." She laughed, while starting to back away.

"Clara! Wait, I need to hear more about this. Are you really going to leave me hanging?"

"Mm hmm. Now, you know how it feels. This time, I'll be the one who's filling you in on the details tonight. And I still want to hear more about your author friend."

Clara continued backing away a couple of steps, winking at Agnes before completely walking away.

"You know what they say about payback, don't you?" Agnes yelled.

"I have no idea what you're talking about."

Agnes waved her off, then left, heading toward the coffee shop.

*Yep, we're sisters from the same mother all right. There's no denying it,* she thought.

Inside the coffee shop, Agnes debated over which dessert would satisfy her craving. *Brownie, danish, or chocolate chip cookie?* she said in a low voice. All the options were very tempting, given that she had a sweet tooth that wouldn't quit nagging her.

"For breakfast?" a man's voice said, startling her from behind. "Surely you want to start your day with something more hardy."

Agnes stopped looking at the mouth-watering case of treats and shifted her attention toward the voice.

"Oh, God." She murmured under her breath.

"Well, good morning to you too. Somebody woke up on the wrong side of the bed as usual," Grant replied.

She was tempted to turn around and pretend like she didn't see him, but it was too late for that. What were the odds that she'd run into him a second time in the same week? *I could've sworn he had a book to finish.*

"Just to be sure I understand this correctly. The last time

we saw each other you were the one who kissed me, and now you're acting like —" He wavered.

"Shh. You don't have to make a public announcement about it," she said, stepping up to the counter. "Good morning, Harvey. How are you?"

"I'm great. Just concerned about Mackenzie and Beth, that's all. I came outside to stand with them for a little while. I know it has to be tough just waiting around to find out how significant the damage is going to be."

"I know, but thankfully they made it out safely. Now, all we can do is hope for the best possible outcome regarding the café."

In her peripheral she could still see an image of Grant staring, waiting for her to finish putting in her order.

"You having your usual latte today?" Harvey grinned.

"Please, and throw in a croissant for me as well."

"Make that two croissants and two lattes. I'll pick up the tab." Grant interrupted.

Agnes' eyes widened, feeling somewhat enraged, although she couldn't explain why. So instead, she raised her hand to her waist and blew her bangs out of the way. "What are you doing?" *It doesn't matter that he's cute. It doesn't matter that he's cute,* she mentally repeated, trying to maintain a tough stance.

After all, she had to uphold her reputation as a New Yorker. Tough exterior, difficult to fool, no nonsense kind of gal.

Grant looked at Harvey, who was placing the croissants in a bag.

"Harvey, have you ever seen anything like this? A guy tries to do something nice and this is the thanks he gets." He ridiculed, but Agnes didn't budge.

Grant leaned in closer to her.

"Look. You're the one who ran off after giving me an unexpected kiss. I should be the one ignoring you. But I'm not. Instead, I'm standing here asking you to at least finish the conversation we started. Is that too much to ask?"

She glanced around, noticing two patrons she normally would see at the café, then locked eyes again with Grant.

"It is too much to ask. I have research to do, and if I'm not mistaken, don't you have a book to write? Mr. Mystery Writer."

Agnes reached in her pocket and pulled out a bill, leaving it on the counter for Harvey.

"I'm paying for the latte and croissant, plus I still owe you for the jacket," she said.

"You don't owe me anything, and I'm not a mystery writer."

"You are to me. I've yet to hear you say one word about what you write." She countered.

"But you're interested in knowing?"

Harvey placed their lattes and a couple of brown paper bags on the counter. He leaned forward and muttered quietly. "This feels like déjà vu. You were just doing this the other night, standing here bickering, like an old married couple."

Agnes could tell that Harvey was quite entertained, but she wasn't as amused.

Grant repositioned himself, folding his arms. "I'm having a hard time figuring you out. Did I say or do something to offend you?"

"No. Not at all."

"Okay. That's good to know," he said.

"I just don't want anyone trying to figure me out. It has absolutely nothing to do with you."

Agnes couldn't help but notice the fresh scent of soap that lingered when he reached past her to pick up his food. He was fit around the waistline, wore a clean haircut, and his overall look was made for the front cover of a magazine.

"Hmm. So, out of the two of us, you're the mysterious one. Not me," Grant, said.

"Call it what you may, but I really need to get to my research. It was nice running into you again," she replied.

"Why are you trying to get away so fast? Sit. Talk with me for a while. If the conversation is that terrible, then I'll never bother you again. I promise."

In the background someone commented loud enough for everyone to hear.

"Lady, please talk to the guy already. You're holding up the line."

Fighting her internal resistance, Agnes stepped out of the line and followed Grant's gesture toward a table. Falling into the old routine of being captivated by the cute guy was a thing of the past, and she really wanted to leave it there.

"There's really no point in doing this. I'm working on business plans and —"

Grant stopped her. "What did he do to you?"

"Excuse me?"

"The guy who broke your heart. What did he do to you? How did it end?" he asked.

She felt her blood boiling, as if there was such a thing. How else could she explain the amount of heat escaping her pores?

"Who does that? I don't think I've ever met anybody who would ask such a question. You don't know me," she said.

"That's because you're making it difficult for me to get to know you. I'll tell you one thing, that's for certain. I'm right. Someone recently broke your heart. The signs are obvious."

"What signs?" she said, letting out a high-pitched tone.

"Oh, I don't know. Let's see. Could it be the constant avoidance?" he asked.

"No, that could simply mean that I'm not interested."

They paused, glaring at each other while still standing next to a table. Neither of them made the first move to sit down.

"I'm not buying that for one minute. You wouldn't have kissed me if there wasn't the slightest bit of interest." He smiled, then laid his latte and croissant on the table.

"Oh, really," she said.

"Between the constant avoidance and your sabbatical, it's clear that you're running from something. So, all I want to know is, who did you wrong?"

"What are you? Some sort of relationship expert?" she asked.

"No, but I'm a romance author. I've written about this sort of thing a time or two. It's the classic case of a woman who's scorned by a man who didn't do right by her."

Feeling exposed, she said nothing at first. Instead, she sipped her coffee, keeping her eyes on him as if waiting for him to finish telling her life story.

"Romance. Hmm. How did you get into that?" She grunted.

"It sort of fell in my lap. I didn't set out to be a writer. I actually thought I was heading toward a promising career in journalism, but things didn't work out as expected. And, since I've always been one to wear my heart on my sleeve, while carrying around my journal... well, put the two together and you have the makings of a romance writer."

Again, they entered a staring contest, this time with Agnes softening the whole tough girl act.

"This conversation would be a lot easier sitting down, you know. I promise I won't bite." He teased.

She thought about it, then caved, allowing him to pull out her chair.

"How about we start over? I'll go first if it will make you feel comfortable."

She waved her hand, giving him the right of way.

"My name is Grant Owings. I'm forty-three, an author, and I'm here visiting Solomons Island for inspiration while finishing up the second half of my novel. I'm originally from Tennessee, but I travel so much that my accent isn't as prevalent. And oh, before I forget, I have a birthmark the size of a golf ball in a place you'd least expect."

Agnes spit out her latte, allowing uncontrollable laughter to take over.

# CHAPTER 5

*J*onathan Middleton rummaged through his toolbox, pulling out the perfect wrench for the job in front of him. Bending down on his knees was no simple task, but once again, the new neighbor, Edith, called him with a household emergency, and although Mae wasn't particularly fond of her, he caved, deciding to take a quick look.

"Jonathan, thank you for going to all this trouble for me. I don't know how the previous owners managed to function in this place. This is about the third appliance that has malfunctioned this month." She complained.

"You don't say."

He wondered if any of these malfunctions came up on her inspection report prior to purchasing the place. Even though, nowadays, people were so focused on making a quick buck, it may have been overlooked.

He emerged from underneath the sink, dabbing his hands on a towel before testing the switch to the disposal.

"Edith, from the looks of things, your disposal is shot. They usually have a lifespan of about ten years, give or take. Either way, if you want to avoid having a leak all over your cabinets and the floor, you'll need to buy a replacement from the hardware store down by Patuxent Beach."

She gasped. "Jonathan. You're probably going to think I'm a complete fool for saying this, but I don't know anything about purchasing a dishwasher disposal. What if I choose the wrong one?" she asked, sounding like a damsel in distress.

Edith stood about five-foot-four, with her hair and nails put together, just so. She wore perfume and was very dainty. Definitely not the kind of woman you would expect to see in a hardware store.

"Don't worry. I'd be happy to write everything down for you. The guys at the store will show you the ropes, and I'm sure they can even recommend a plumber who can do the install for you." He suggested.

"A plumber? I thought you said you know how to fix it? I'm new to the island and it's hard knowing who you can trust to come into your home these days."

"I know, but you don't have to —" She cut him off right in the middle of his excuse to head back home.

"Please, Jonathan? I'll repay you. And, if you take me with you to the hardware store, I can even make a nice pot of my famous lobster bisque when we get back. What do you say?" She batted her eyes.

Jonathan nearly choked on his own saliva.

"No, no. You're too kind, but that won't be necessary, Edith."

"You're not a fan of lobster, are you?" She suggested.

"I love a good bowl of lobster bisque, it's not that at all. It's just —"

He looked at her puppy dog expression, feeling awful that he was about to tell her no. But he also knew in the back of his mind that if this project turned into anything more than a quick fix, Mae would probably chew him up for breakfast, lunch, and dinner.

"It's Mae. I promised her when she gets back from getting her hair done that I'd help with dinner. I'd hate to keep her waiting."

Edith looked around the kitchen counter at all the products she'd cleared from the cabinet underneath the sink. As he watched her, he could see himself standing at a fork in the road, knowing no matter which route he chose, the outcome probably would not be good. Let's face it, he was already in her house, standing in the midst of her kitchen after his wife expressed ill feelings toward the woman.

Against his better judgement, he proceeded. "Ahh, what the heck. If we go now, we can be back within a half an hour, tops. I'll switch out the disposal for you, but then I have to be on my way."

"Thank you, Jonathan. Thank you, thank you, thank you." She went on.

"Yeah, sure. While we're down there, I'm going to introduce you to the owner and ask him if he can suggest a handyman. I'm sure Paul will know someone you can trust."

"I'd appreciate it," she said, happily.

The sound of her voice reminded him of a woman he knew back in his college days. She was around the same height and beautiful like Edith, but always dated the more popular guys in their class.

"Edith, in the few times I've been over here, I don't recall you saying anything about your hometown. Where are you from?" he asked.

"Annapolis."

"Get out. So am I. I was born and raised in Annapolis. We may have crossed paths a time or two and don't even know it." He beamed.

"I grew up by the Harbour Center. Are you familiar with the area?"

"Am I? I have an old pal, Dock, that runs a marina over there. Every once in a while, Mae and I like to take a day trip up and steal away on one of his yachts."

"That's sounds so romantic," she replied.

"Yeah, it sort of became a thing we like to do in the summer just to get away. But, uh. What were we talking about again?"

"Where we grew up."

"Yes, that's right. I grew up not too far away from the Naval Academy. I have fond memories of those days, spending practically all of my childhood on a boat."

"Sure, I know the area very well. I have friends who still live there." She smiled, relaxing back against the counter.

"It's such a small world. I wouldn't be surprised if we didn't know some of the same people."

"You never know. I bet if we pull out our yearbooks, we'd be pleasantly surprised." She chuckled.

"Yearbook? That's funny. I haven't seen mine in ages. I don't know that I want to see it either. Back in my school days, I was a tall and boney little fella. Picture day was my least favorite day of the school year." Jonathan found himself laughing so hard until he straightened up and cleared his throat.

"So, what brings you to Solomons Island?" he asked.

"Gee, where do I begin? Do you have time to grab a cup of coffee on the way to the hardware store?"

He glanced over at her clock, remembering the responsible thing to do was to fix the disposal and go.

"Not really. We better get going. Mae and I usually eat dinner around a certain time, and I don't want to keep her waiting," he said.

"Of course. What was I thinking?"

"It's okay. How about I give you a moment to gather your things while I put my tools in the back of the truck?"

"Okay, sure. I'll be right out. Oh, and Jonathan," she said.

"Yes."

"Since you asked... I moved here to start a new chapter. A fresh start, if you will."

He knew it was the perfect moment to accept her general statement without probing any further, but it intrigued him.

"A fresh start from what?"

"A divorce. My husband left me." She chuckled nervously. "Thirty long years of marriage down the drain and now I'm here. Flying solo for now, at least. Hoping not to spend the rest of my days alone." She concluded, leaving Jonathan speechless.

Mackenzie stood, facing the water by the warehouse, allowing her hair to blow in the March wind. Watching the water was her form of meditation as she waited for Brody to join her. She had four weeks ahead of her to wait for the contractors to complete repairs at the café. And four long weeks to pinch a few pennies together, making sure she paid all the bills and continued providing for her daughter.

"There she is," Brody said as he approached.

"Hey, love. I see you were finally able to break free."

"Yes, I was slammed for about an hour. Trying to balance my regular job and helping here at the warehouse has been a little tricky, but we're making it work," he said.

She felt the warmth of his mouth pressing against hers with a sweet kiss, easing the anxiety she was feeling. After about a minute, he stopped and began massaging her shoulders.

"Are you okay?"

"I'm going to be fine. I know I will. But, I'm a worrier at

heart. It's in my DNA to have everything all figured out, and this fire really turned all of my careful planning upside down," she replied.

"Babe, I'll say it as many times as I need to. You and Stephanie have a place to stay. All you have to do is say the word, and it's done."

"I know. Thank you, Brody. It means the world to me that you would do that for us. But I'm the one who made the decision to move full speed ahead with leasing the café. And I'm the one who's responsible for ensuring Stephanie's stability. If I move her out of our place to save a little money, it's only a temporary solution. Plus, her commute to school would be even further away. I'm going to have to tough this one out, that's all. Hey, putting things in proper perspective, it could've been worse, right?"

He brushed her hair out of the way with his fingers.

"Yes, you're right. But seeing the walls blackened with smoke and having water damage is no fun either. I'm just glad you all made it out safely. I'm also glad to hear the owner and the insurance company are doing all they can to get the place up and running as soon as possible," he said.

"So am I. There's more than just my livelihood at stake here. Dakota and Joshua need their paychecks just as much as I do."

Brody positioned himself behind her, wrapping his arms around her waist.

"I trust your judgement when it comes to you and Steph. But you need to know that I'm here for you. Anything you guys need, and I mean anything, just ask me. Whatever you do, please don't allow pride to get in the way," he said.

"Is that what you think of me, Brody? You think I'm prideful?"

He turned her around again.

"I think you are a strong woman who's accustomed to fighting her own battles and doing things on her own. I can't blame you for that. The man who was supposed to be by your side bailed, leaving you with no other option. But now you have me. I know I'm not Steph's dad. But I'm growing to love your girl as if she were my very own. God knows I love you, Mack. So, please. Take what I said the right way. It's coming straight from the heart."

"I know. I've always been a little too stubborn for my own good. Yet again, another trait in my DNA." She giggled.

"I wouldn't say stubborn. It's more like determined. Determined to stand tall and strong for you and Steph and to make a good life for the two of you. The only difference is now you have somebody to lean on... if you choose," he said.

"I like the way that sounds."

"Good. I was hoping you would. Now, we have the next four weeks to map out plans for the future. But, for now, there's somebody I'd like for you to meet." Brody extended his hand toward her.

There was something about his mannerisms and his gentleman-like ways that made her quiver, but she tried not to let it show.

"Right now?" she asked.

"Yep. They're waiting up at the warehouse for us. I hope you don't mind, but since I knew you'd be stopping by, I figured it might be a good time for you to meet somebody."

"Brody, what are you up to? I didn't come dressed for a meeting. Yoga pants don't hardly qualify as meeting attire."

He helped her step over a rocky area and then looked her square in the eyes.

"Mackenzie, you effortlessly make all of your clothing look good. Especially yoga pants. Now, come with me. This is one meeting that you really don't want to miss."

# CHAPTER 6

*A*gnes Covington ignored the sound of her cell phone ringing in her back pocket while approaching the boat slip. In just a couple of hours, she'd head down to the warehouse and talk to Mike about her new position. But, for now, the tranquil views of the Patuxent from Clara's backyard helped put her mind at ease. It was exactly what she needed as she thought about her next steps for planting deeper roots on Solomons Island.

The sound of a nearby waterfall captivated her attention, causing her to close her eyes and give in to the sweet serenity of it all, when her phone rang again.

"Oh, for Pete's sake," she said out loud. "Hello."

"I was hoping I had the right number. How are you? It's me, Grant."

She covered her forehead with one hand, remembering that she caved and gave him her number, feeling somewhat of a social obligation to do so, since he'd been kind enough to sit and talk to her in the coffee shop. She didn't believe it would lead to anything. And certainly, she didn't expect him to call.

"Grant. Hi."

"Did I catch you at a bad time?"

"No, not really. I was just hanging out back in the great outdoors, organizing my thoughts, before heading into work."

"Oh, so you were able to get a job, after all?" he asked.

"You could call it that. My soon to be brother-in-law needs some help at his company and well, I need a job, so—"

"That's great, as long as you're happy. Do I detect a little uncertainty in your voice?" he asked.

"No. Not at all. I think the job is going to be perfect. More like a blessing in disguise because it will allow me the flexibility I need to get the food truck up and running."

"That's right. The food truck. I'm happy for you. To think that just a few days ago you were upset about losing your position at the restaurant. Now look." He chuckled.

"Yeah."

The line fell silent.

"I ... I just called to let you know I had a nice time talking to you the other day. The conversation was rather pleasant," he said.

"Yeah, about that, Grant. I agree with you but—"

"Hold on. Let me guess. You're going to tell me that although you agree, it's a bad time, or you're too busy, or something like it," he replied.

"Well, it wouldn't be a lie. You kind of caught me at a bad time. I'm still trying to find my footing here in Solomons. And, somehow, although hearing interesting stories about your life as a traveling writer is very intriguing, I think you're just as busy as I am. Just a few chapters away from packing your bags and leaving, if I'm not mistaken."

Grant cleared his throat on the other end of the line.

"Am I to assume you gave me your number because you're not interested in talking to me?" He inquired.

She felt a small jab on the inside of her stomach. He had her there. Feelings of attraction crept up in the most unexpected way. Plus, she was curious, maybe even a little into him.

"What can I say? We were having coffee, the conversation was good, and when you asked me, I didn't want to be rude. But, if I'm being honest with myself, the timing is terrible. For both of us."

"Yeah, and then there's your sabbatical and all. Wouldn't want to forget about that." He teased.

"Ha ha, funny guy. Keep it up and you'll find yourself listening to the dial tone."

"Okay, okay. I'm sorry. Please don't hang up. Instead, I want you to make a deal with me." He waited.

"I'm listening."

"You're not dating right now, and you have a new business to focus on. I, on the other hand, need to stay on track, meeting my deadlines with my publisher," he said.

"Mm hmm."

"But that doesn't mean we don't need an occasional break, spending time thinking about something other than work."

"And?" She probed.

"And if we need an occasional break, I don't see why we can't get together every once in a while and laugh, hopefully taking our mind off things. I'll be honest, it does wonders for me. Every time we talk, I'm able to go back and write just as if my writer's block didn't exist."

"Oh, now I see what this is really about. You're using me so you can finish writing your book!" She chuckled, while picking up a rock and throwing it into the water.

"I wouldn't call it that at all. But, I do enjoy your company. And, I'm glad we finally had a chance to sit down and talk, instead of always being so hit or miss. Come on, Agnes. Please.

You know what they say about all work and no play." He begged.

She waited, holding her breath for ten intentional seconds before exhaling.

"Fine. But it's just for the next couple of weeks until the dust settles with my new job and you finish your book. And, for the record, I am still on my sabbatical, and there will be no more kissing. Got it?"

"Yes, ma'am. Just friends. Sabbatical is still in full effect. Copy. Although, as your friend, we really need to dive more into this topic. I'm dying to know the details of what led an attractive woman like yourself into a sabbatical in the first place."

"Yeah, we'll dive in all right. Starting right after you divulge more about your books and about this mysterious life of traveling you've created for yourself. Packing up and moving around from place to place, never settling down. Sounds like I'm not the only one running," she said, practically daring him.

"Okay. Tonight, I have a virtual meeting, but let's say tomorrow evening around seven. Meet me at the little restaurant over by Stoney Point. Dinner is on me and before you say anything, it's not a date. I'm just creating an atmosphere where we can talk. Are you in?"

She threw another rock and watched a ripple form in the water.

"I'll see you at seven," she said.

# CHAPTER 7

*J*onathan rolled under the hood of his truck, checking for the source of a leak he'd spotted the day prior. He wasn't afraid to get dirty, but he also knew his expertise only went but so far before he'd have to put a call in to the local mechanic. So far, he was content with a few tools by his side, hoping the problem would be minor.

He loosened a few bolts with his wrench, checking the oil drain plug ever so carefully. In the background, he could hear the garage door opening and slamming shut, causing him to shift his gaze, which then caused oil to drip all over his hand.

"Darn it." He complained.

"Having trouble fixing the truck, dear?"

"No. I haven't made a whole lot of progress to begin with. Just fiddling around, that's all. Would you pass me one of the rags on the counter, Mae? I need to clean up a little spill."

He watched her feet walk around to his workbench, then return, passing along a couple of his rags.

"You know, Jonathan. I've been meaning to talk to you. I wanted to go over our itinerary for the trip we're planning in

April. The grands are excited about spending their spring break on the boat with us, and I just want to do everything we possibly can to make the trip special," she said.

"It will be, Mae. We can go over everything later on this weekend. Right now, I have oil dripping everywhere, and I've yet to figure out what the problem is here."

"That's fine. I can pull up a chair and keep you company. Let's see. Where was I? Oh, I spoke to Lily, and she was wondering if we'd consider sailing down to the North Carolina shoreline. She said something about Emerald Isle being a nice place to visit for vacation. What do you think?" Mae asked.

"I know nothing about Emerald Isle, Mae. I'd have to look into it. Plus, you know me, I'm not fussy. Whatever will appease you and the kids is what I want to do."

"Mm hmm. In my heart of hearts, I'd like to continue further down to Georgia. I've heard so much about Tybee Island. I can see it now, crossing right over the Savannah River and sailing in, docking at a beautiful marina, and enjoying all the delicious food the island offers." She sighed. "Dreamy. Simply dreamy."

Jonathan grunted while Mae couldn't stop herself from dreaming. "Well, perhaps we should hold off and save that trip for the summer. I'm sure we can talk to Mike about taking a couple of weeks off. That way, we'd have more freedom and flexibility."

"Mae. I wouldn't get too far ahead of yourself on making summer plans just yet. Let's see how the first trip goes, then we can talk about the summer. This will be our first time setting sail on a family vacation. Don't want to be too overzealous," he said, then rolled from under the truck.

Standing about five-foot-eight feet tall and wearing denim overalls, working in the garage made Jonathan feel useful, just like his dad was when he was a child.

"Overzealous? That's an interesting choice of words. Last summer, you couldn't wait to purchase a boat. I specifically recall you saying just about anything you could to talk me into the idea. Now, I'm being overzealous?" She demanded.

"No, Mae. Not really. It's just a figure of speech. All I'm saying is we have time. Let's see how the first trip goes and if it's a success, then we can talk about sailing to Georgia, or wherever else you want to go."

He looked over at his wife sitting on one of the high stools he often used in the garage. Her legs were crossed, and she was draped in one of her beautiful house dresses. One that gave his heart a jolt every time he saw her in it.

"Hmm. Jonathan, I wish you would tell me what's really swirling around in that head of yours. Whatever it is, you haven't been acting like yourself lately. It's like you're pre-occupied or something."

All thoughts of her beautiful dress fizzled. Instead, he began looking for his case that contained multiple drill bits.

"Mae, there's nothing wrong with me. I came out here to have a peaceful afternoon fixing my truck, that's all. Nothing more. Nothing less."

She closed the brochure she was holding in her hand and made direct eye contact with Jonathan. "Are you sure about that? Your mood always seems to shift after visiting with Edith. I know you were over there yesterday, Jonathan. I saw your truck in her driveway on the way home from the salon. The only reason I didn't come over and personally give her a piece of my mind was because I saw the front door was cocked open halfway."

"What's that supposed to mean?" he asked, sounding irritated.

"Jonathan Middleton. I'm not the one who deserves to be

questioned here. Why didn't you say anything to me? One would think you have a few secrets of your own."

He groaned, then placed his tool set down on the counter and faced her. "She came over here with a leak emergency. What was I to do, being put in such an awkward position? If it means anything to you, I took her to the hardware store and introduced her to the owner, ensuring that he recommend a handyman she could call on for any future problems. It was all innocent, I swear."

"You took her in your car? I can hear it now. If anybody saw you together, we'll be the talk of the island."

"Oh, Mae, for heaven's sake. This is getting way too far out of hand. You know you're the only woman for me. It doesn't matter how beautiful the woman looks —"

He held his forehead, immediately regretting his choice of words. Jonathan's desire was truly for Mae only, but he was going to have a hard time convincing her after admitting that Edith was beautiful.

Mackenzie pulled into the carpool line at Stephanie's school. It was tradition to exchange hugs, pass her daughter a hot thermos lunch, and wish her a good day before heading to the café. This morning would be no exception, especially since she was eager to see the initial phase of work started by the contractors.

"Mom, will we have to pack our things and leave Solomons Island?" Stephanie asked.

"Sweetheart, what would make you ask such a thing?"

"Will we?"

"Stephanie, of course not. I wouldn't keep something like that a secret from you."

"That's what the kids at school are saying. They're talking

about us having no money because of the fire at the café. One kid, Sean, says it's just a matter of time before we have to pack our bags and leave the island for good."

Mackenzie shifted the gear into park, completely ignoring the beeping horns behind her.

"Listen to me, sweet girl. Sure, anytime you endure something like a fire, it can be a setback. But, in our case, we got lucky. We're going to be just fine. We have insurance money to cover the damage, Sweetheart. In another four weeks mommy will be back to work and everything will be back to normal."

Stephanie's mouth drooped and a teardrop fell down her cheek.

"Baby, you believe Mommy, don't you?"

"Yes, it's just the kids at school keep teasing me. At first, I tried to ignore them, but it's making me feel sad." She explained.

"Well, maybe I ought to call a meeting with your teacher. Surely she can help get to the bottom of things and prevent the other kids from teasing you ever again."

Stephanie nodded her head up and down.

"That's not the only thing they're making fun of me for."

Mack shifted the gear, pulling out of line into a parking space. Once the car was in park, she cut the engine off and faced Stephanie.

"What else are they saying, love?" She urged.

After letting out a heart-wrenching sob, Stephanie managed to continue.

"They make fun of me because I don't have a real dad. They say I like to pretend that Brody is my dad because my real dad doesn't want me anymore." Once the words left her mouth, the remaining tears flowed like an endless stream.

Mackenzie's heart raced, weighing whether to march right into the school and give the staff a piece of her mind. *How did these kids have so much time on their hands to tease Stephanie the way they did? Weren't they supposed to be learning and engaging in productive activity?* she thought. But in the end, she knew better. She knew it wasn't the teacher's fault.

She reached into the glove department for a box of tissues.

"Baby girl, listen to me. Those kids don't know what they're talking about."

"But it's true, dad doesn't care about me. That's why he left when I was a baby," she said, still sniffling.

Mackenzie received her words like a gut-wrenching blow to the stomach. At the end of the day, she couldn't explain why her dad turned out to be such a deadbeat father. Or why traveling the world and joining a band was ten times more appealing than being around to raise his own flesh and blood. The only thing she knew to do at this moment was to be honest with Stephanie.

"I wish Mommy could explain why your father made the choices he did, but I can't, baby. The only thing that gives me peace is seeing how much of a beautiful family we still are, although your father is not with us. If you ask me, I think we live a pretty good life together as a mother and daughter team. And, having Brody around... well, that's like having—"

"The cherry on top of an ice cream sundae?" Stephanie interrupted.

"Yes. That's exactly what I was thinking." She leaned across the console and gripped Stephanie, giving her the tightest bear hug she could.

"Mom, I can't breathe." Steph giggled.

"I'm sorry." She held Stephanie by the shoulders instead. "I just need to know that you're okay. Unfortunately, sometimes kids will say mean things. Promise me you won't let it crush your little spirit."

"I won't."

"And, Steph."

"Yes, Mommy."

"You have more power than you know, love. If the mean kids ever tease you again, get up and walk away. Only spend time around the kids you can trust and go tell a teacher. It's their job to help you," Mackenzie said, rubbing her head and consoling her.

"Okay."

"Good. I'm going to reach out to your teacher. But for now. I have a really fun idea."

"What is it?"

"How about today you go to school for a half day? I'll swing by and pick you up right after lunch. I have to stop by the café for about an hour, but maybe we can surprise Brody after and beg him to join us for sundaes. Besides, I owe him a big thank you for doing something special for me."

"Sundaes always help me feel better," Stephanie replied.

"Me too. Of course, we can't make this a habit, but for today, do we have a deal?"

"We definitely have a deal. And, while I'm at school, if those kids bother me, I promise to tell Mrs. Jennings."

Mack grabbed her, kissing her on the forehead.

"That's what I like to hear. Now, let's get you checked in before the bell rings."

With the inventory checklist complete, Mackenzie wandered through the café, eyeing everything one last time. The contractors had begun demolition work in the kitchen, and she figured the rest of the place could use a thorough cleaning from a local service, or perhaps her personalized touch, since she had nothing to do over the next several weeks.

"Don't even think about it," Clara said, peering her head in through the front door.

Mackenzie jumped.

"Ooh, girl, you almost startled me to death. What are you doing sneaking up on me like that?"

"The real question is what are you doing here? I just happened to be cleaning the front window over at Lighthouse Tours when I saw your car parked out front. Does Brody know you're here?"

Mackenzie looked beyond Clara's shoulder, pointing in her direction.

"Well, I guess he does now. Look behind you."

The front door opened again, this time Brody pressing through, with a couple of bags in hand. Somehow, even after over a year of dating, her adrenaline always seemed to spike whenever she saw him coming her way. It was probably his muscular physique that did it to her.

"I thought I saw a little activity through the front window. Ladies," he said, tipping his baseball cap.

"Hey, babe. I was going to stop by after I finished taking inventory and assessing everything that still needs to be done," she said, waving her hands around, then flopping them at her side.

Brody didn't appear to be too pleased by the idea.

"You two do realize that you're standing in the middle of a work zone, right? One that hasn't necessarily been deemed safe for the public. For all we know, we could be breathing in toxins from the fire."

Mackenzie's eyebrows crinkled, feeling a little less anxious about it.

"Well, if it's safe enough for the guys to come here and work, I'm not sure that it's such a big deal. Besides, somebody needs to tend to the rest of the café, washing it down from top to bottom, don't you think?"

Clara giggled, then cleared her throat.

"Mack, that's what the insurance money is for. It's their job to provide enough funds to pay for all the services you will need to get this place up and running again. You need to relax, friend. Take this time at home to make big plans for your grand re-opening," she said.

Brody chimed in.

"Now, that's a good idea. You've always been creative. Dream up something big. Design a grand-opening sign. You can even create flyers, but whatever you do, do it outside of this place until the professionals tell us it's safe. That includes you as well, Ms. Clara. I'm sure if Mike knew you were over here, he'd have a cow." He smiled.

"You'll get no arguments out of me. On that note, Mack, you need to follow me. It's been a while since we had time to catch up. Come over to Lighthouse Tours for a little while. We can bundle up and head out by the dock while I share the latest news with you." Clara smiled.

Brody chimed in again. "Yes, quality girlfriend time, anything to get her mind off this place. Go... have fun!" he said, extending his hand to escort her outside.

Mackenzie had to admit, the impromptu visit from Clara uplifted her spirit and some girlfriend time would help take her mind off the renovations, even if only for a little while.

"Ooh, and I can tell you about the interview I had yesterday with a reporter from Solomons Daily," she said, while following everyone out and locking the front door.

"Really? How did you land an interview with Solomons Daily?" Clara asked.

"I owe it all to Brody. He set it up for me. They're going to do a feature on the café, honoring the history of the place, and how it's noted as the most popular gathering spot for the people of Solomons."

"That's amazing." Clara shifted her attention to Brody. "Nice job, sir. Getting an interview with them is no easy task. I hear they can be really selective over there. Good for you," she said, giving him a friendly slap on the shoulder.

"Thanks. Trust me, if it wasn't for the historical nature of the café, I'm almost certain they would've said no. Either way, I'm just happy to see something positive come of this, that's all."

"Agreed," Mack said. "Okay, we better get a move on if I'm going to catch up with you for a little while. I have to pick Stephanie up around twelve, and then I promised her I'd bring her by the warehouse so she could see you, Brody. If that's okay with you? She was having a rough morning, and I thought a little ice cream sundae might do her some good. Honestly, it might do us all some good."

He stepped closer, planting his lips on Mackenzie's. "You never have to ask me. I always look forward to a visit from you and Steph. I'll see you this afternoon?" he asked.

*Is it normal to have such a crush?* she thought to herself. Whether it was or not, Brody was doing something to her that she couldn't deny.

"All right, you two. I'll give you a moment to say your good-byes. Brody, you tell my sister I'm coming down there to check on her. She better be doing a good job." Clara teased.

"She's doing an excellent job. You'd be proud."

Agnes pulled down the cobblestone drive leading to the little restaurant at Stoney Point, just as Grant had described. *This is not a date*, she told herself. However, if she was being honest, it was incredibly difficult to decide what to wear, how to do her hair, and whether she should put on perfume for her non-date. It was the very reason she thought men and women could never just be friends. There was always some element of attraction or curiosity between the two. *Wasn't there?*

Inside, she spotted Grant seated at a corner table over-looking the river. Her heart wasn't supposed to be thumping uncontrollably, but it was, and there was no way to regain control over it at this point. So, she took the first steps, ignoring her feelings, refusing to accept that they were real.

"Agnes?" he said, looking somewhat surprised.

*He invited me he, didn't he?* she thought.

"Wow. You look — you look stunning. I guess I should've put on something a little less casual," he said, brushing off his pants.

"Not at all. I don't get out nearly as much as I should. If I did, then I'd actually know how to dress for occasions like this," she said, laughing it off.

"You look perfect. I wanted to make sure I honored your wishes, not making it feel like a date. I was actually looking over the menu before you arrived. There are so many delicious options, I hardly know where to begin," he said. "Why don't you have a seat, stay a while, and keep me company?" He pulled out her chair, then joined her on the other side of the table.

"Thank you."

Agnes watched as a waitress passed by with a large pizza pan, leaving behind an aroma to die for.

"Would you like to order a large pie that we can split? I can go for a pepperoni slice any day of the week," he said.

"Was I that obvious?"

"I won't say obvious, but you only live once, right? Might as well go for what makes you happy. Besides, I too am a pizza lover, and I've heard this place does an amazing rendition of wood-fired pizza. We may as well give it a try. What do you say?" he asked.

"Okay, sure. One large oven fired pizza and maybe a soda on the side."

"I like the sound of that."

He signaled their server to the table, allowing time for Agnes to observe every gesture and every movement he made. Why was she so curious about this guy? A man she hardly knew.

"Okay, so I've been dying to ask you how things are going at the new job. Did you start yet?" he asked.

*Dying to know? Interesting choice of words,* she thought.

"Uh, yeah. Sort of. This week, Mike and Brody have been showing me the ropes. There's not much to it at this point. Check the system to stay on top of billing notices, help a customer check their boat out, it's not too hard. The thing I'm enjoying most is the opportunity to work on my business plans when it's quiet. It's a sweet deal, if you ask me."

"Nice. And, speaking of your business, when can the people of Solomons expect the food truck to be up and running?" he asked.

"If all goes well, by June. I'm pretty pumped about it, actually. The kids will almost be out of school, which means that parents will be ready to travel, and local tourism will be booming with people ready to experience the island. That's when I plan to hit them with The Barbecue Hut."

He relaxed in his chair, smiling at the idea.

"The Barbecue Hut, huh? Okay. Nice. I guess I'll have to circle back this summer and come check out The Barbecue Hut, unless you want to give me an early sample. I could be your official guinea pig."

She chuckled.

"What? I'm being serious. A man has to eat while pushing

through the last part of his novel, and you need to make sure you're not about to become the laughingstock of Solomons Island. I'm just trying to spare you by giving an early and honest review."

Dimples emerged on Agnes' cheeks as she noticed the clever way in which he was trying to become one of her first customers. After the laughter settled down, his hand rested on hers, to which she felt an undeniable surge between them.

"All jokes aside, I'd love to show my support in some way. When I come back to visit, I promise to be the first in line to check out your business."

She nervously pulled her hand back to her side of the table.

"Thank you, and if you ever tell me the title of your book, I promise I'll be one of the first to purchase a copy," she replied.

"I'll tell you what. I'll sign a copy and send it to you directly."

"Wow, you mean the mysterious romance writer is willing to reveal his precious work to me? I feel special."

"You should. It's not often that I befriend strangers who dowse me in coffee. I'm just saying." Grant teased.

The fresh sizzling pizza was delivered to their table along with plates and additional napkins.

"Can I get anything else for you?" the waiter asked.

"Outside of our drinks, I think we're good," he responded, referencing Agnes to be sure.

She nodded.

"I'm sorry, we're so busy this evening. I should've had your drinks on the table by now. I'll be right back."

Agnes picked up her fork and knife, trying to properly remove a slice from the tray on to her plate.

"Oh, goodness. Please tell me you're not one of those kind," he said.

"What?"

"The only way... and I mean it when I say the only way to eat pizza is to pick it up with your hands and dig in. None of this formal, gingerly cutting it with a knife nonsense. Didn't you say you were from New York? I think New Yorkers like to fold their pizza up and go for it, the last time I checked." He demonstrated with his slice, catching the dripping mozzarella with his tongue.

"I was getting there. Besides, you should be careful with the generalizations, buddy. I'm sure there are some New Yorkers who prefer eating their pizza with a fork and knife." She playfully scolded.

"Yeah, well, I have an aunt who lives there and if she saw the move you just pulled, she'd definitely have something to say about it."

She nodded her head, feeling somewhat relieved at the invitation to drop the formalities. It wasn't her style anyway, and she wasn't sure why she cared enough to be anything other than herself.

Grant groaned after a couple of bites, seemingly pleased with their selection.

"So, regarding your book," she said.

"Mmm."

"Have they fallen in love yet?"

"Who?" he asked.

"Your couple. I would imagine the ultimate goal in a romance novel is to have the couple fall in love, right?"

"Yes, of course." He inhaled, swallowing the last bite before further explaining.

"My main character has finally come to her senses, realizing if she doesn't let her guard down and take a chance on love, she may miss out on something wonderful. It probably doesn't help that he's about to pack his things and leave for good, given that he's the CEO of a major company in another country, but still. She has a decision to make, and I think she'll do the right thing," he said with a proud smile.

"Hmm. Interesting."

She put her crust down, wiping her mouth with a napkin. Normally the crust was the grand finale. The finishing touch. But, his storyline had her intrigued for not so good reasons.

"Go ahead, tell me what's on your mind," he said.

"Nothing. Absolutely nothing."

"Agnes, come on. I detect a small hint of agitation in your voice. What is it?" He pressed.

"Do you really want to know?"

"Yes and no, given that I'm this close to finishing my book. But, go ahead. Give it to me, anyway."

"Okay. I can't help but wonder why the woman has to be the one to give up everything for him. I mean, what if she's already sacrificed enough by just accepting him into her life. That's the problem with love today. It's way too lopsided. Mainly with the woman being loyal and dedicated, giving everything she has to make it work, only for him to turn around and disappoint her in some major way. Like cheating for instance." She explained, crinkled brows and an expression of disdain across her face.

"Hmm. You're right. That is interesting. And, it sounds personal, I might add."

Her eyes rolled toward the scenic views instead of giving him a response.

"Please. Go on. I'd like to hear more. You're basically telling me my main character shouldn't pack her bags and join her forever love, even though he adores her, practically worships the ground she walks on, just because of, what reason again?" he asked.

"Now look at who's being personal."

She murmured under her breath, wishing she hadn't dug a

hole to climb out of. Maybe her feelings were personal, but she had been through a lot. She could name countless situations where she was dedicated, giving her all, and still got the raw end of the deal in the end.

"What do I know? I'm sure your happy ending will be just fine, giving the readers exactly what they want to hear," she said.

He snickered.

"If only I could chip away at that outer layer of yours. I'd bet money there's a diamond in the rough somewhere below the surface, waiting to be exposed."

"What's that supposed to mean? I'm not one of your characters, you know. I'm a real person who's been through some real things. Things I'm not too proud of and other things I simply didn't deserve."

"My characters' lives are based on actual stories. Stories of people just like yourself, Agnes. The thing is... at some point, you have to realize that not everyone you meet is out to do you wrong. Not everyone is going to exhibit behaviors like the men of your past. Some guys, like myself for example. We look at you and we see something special. We just want to get to know you. That's it. Is that too much to ask?"

He reached over, pulling another slice of pizza from the pie and placing it on her plate.

"Here. Eat up before the pizza gets cold," he said, in the most kind way.

"Thank you."

She had to admit that not only was he sexy, but she enjoyed listening to his point of view. Now, if she could just ignore the sensation of butterflies fluttering around in her stomach, then she might view him as a friend only, which was the end goal.

"Listen, I'm sure your readers will love your novel. I just find it hard to follow romantic storylines with a happily ever after ending these days. For me, it's the furthest thing from reality." She sighed.

"That's because you haven't met the right one to help make it your reality. The moment you do, you'll change your tune. But you might want to start by putting on a friendly smile when someone says hello. They say that smiling really goes a long way. Oh, and that whole thing with dowsing hot coffee on guys? Yeah, you've got to let that one go."

They chuckled together over his last point.

"All right. Enough with the coffee already. It was an accident," she said.

"I know. I'm just teasing you."

Grant had a smile that lit up the room, and outside of the stress that came along with meeting his deadlines, he seemed to be carefree. She enjoyed that about him.

At the conclusion of their meal, he took two to-go boxes, dividing the remaining slices between the two of them. Outside, she breathed in the scent of the water while strolling alongside Grant to her car. If he was pursuing her, it would've been a beautiful first date, but she didn't want to think along those lines.

"Will I see you again?" he asked, reaching for the handle of her car door.

"If seeing me means hang out again sometime, sure. I don't see why not," she said.

"Right. I haven't forgotten about the whole hanging out thing." He laughed.

Then he continued. "I was wondering one last thing before I let you go."

Standing within close proximity as he reached for her car door was about to send her into yet another tailspin. She caught another whiff of his cologne.

"What was that?" she asked, biting her lower lip.

"This may seem sort of direct, but tell me again, why did you kiss me that night?"

She closed her eyes, trying to sort out an explanation.

"I already told you, I wasn't thinking clearly —"

"I know what you told me, but what was the real reason?"

Agnes flailed her hands around, explaining her whole sabbatical ordeal when the sweetest and softest lips touched hers.

He kissed her fully, making it last, then withdrew ever so slightly, waiting for a reaction. She could still feel the warmth of his breath on her mouth. Her natural instinct led her to lean in for more, this time not letting go or running away.

# CHAPTER 8

$\mathcal{T}$he next evening, Agnes accompanied Clara and Mackenzie on the deck, sitting on lounge chairs with blankets covered up to their waist. The spring-like weather was slowly making an appearance during the day, but by nightfall it was chilly, making it a good atmosphere for blankets plus an outdoor fireplace.

Holly, Clara's dog, lazily nestled at her feet. Everyone else stargazed for a while, enjoying each other's company.

"I need more nights like this in my life." Mackenzie admitted. "It's the peace and tranquility of living by the water that does it every time for me."

"I know, right? If only we could be so lucky to inherit such a place. You really have it made, sis." Agnes declared.

Clara raised in an upright position.

"Okay. I think it's time we had a real talk about my inheritance from Joan. It's time to set the record straight," Clara said.

"Did I hit a nerve? It was meant to be a compliment," Agnes replied.

"I understand, but this is a very sensitive topic for me.

Everyone seems to think that just because I inherited money and a lovely home from Joan that I must live a luxurious lifestyle or that somehow things have changed for me. And, although they have in some ways, in a lot of other ways, they haven't."

"Not sure that I'm tracking." Mackenzie interrupted.

"Well, for one, I locked away most of the money she left me in a retirement fund, only leaving out enough to make sure I can take care of maintaining this place. I depend on my full-time income from my job just like everyone else. Mack, you of all people should remember my job-hunting days more than anyone else. I used to kick myself back then for being in my forties with absolutely no savings, starting life and my career over from scratch. Remember?"

"I do. That was a trying time for sure," she responded.

"Yes, but Clara, you obviously made it through that rough patch, coming out stronger and even more prosperous than you were before. I'm proud of you, sis. To be honest, I look up to you—" Agnes reached out, squeezing her sister's hand, flashing her a little smile.

It was true. The first day Agnes arrived on her doorstep, she was a hot mess, desperately seeking to put her life back in order. Clara was an example of everything she'd hoped to become someday.

Mackenzie became weepy. "You two make me wish I had a sister. You've come so far in your relationship. It must be nice having someone in your life to talk to like that. Just thinking about it makes me wish —"

Clara interrupted, placing her hand on her arm. "Nope, not allowed. Agnes and I are your sisters, so you don't have to wish for anything. We're also your girlfriends. Speaking of which, we gathered here tonight because we were craving some serious girl time. I think it's absolutely absurd that I live with you,

Agnes, and never see you. And the same goes for you, Mack. Ever since the fire, it has reduced us to quick visits in passing. I miss you," Clara said, in a sentimental tone.

Agnes flung back her blanket, causing the dog to stand at full attention, perking her ears up.

"Let's make a pact once and for all. Let's agree to meet here every week. Same place, same time. With a different bottle of wine, because this one tastes awful."

Laughter erupted, but there had to be some truth to it because no one was touching the wine.

She continued. "Seriously, getting together like this is a proven stress reliever, and it will give us something to look forward to. Not that you two need it. You already have amazing men in your lives." Her voice tapered off.

Mack chimed in. "Honey, not everything revolves around a man. Sure, Brody is a great guy. No doubt about it. But, now that I have all of this extra time on my hands, I find that I'm either bored, nervous about the deadline to re-open, or sad. Sometimes all the above."

Again, Clara reached out to her dear friend. "Mack. Don't be sad. Everything is going to be just fine."

Agnes' level of excitement caught their attention. "See. That's what I'm talking about. We need this. A safe space to talk, to get things off our chest, to be women, and scream at the top of our lungs if we desire!"

"It sounds like you're the one who needs this just as much as the rest of us. What's going on with you? Is everything okay at the warehouse?" Clara asked.

Agnes Covington slumped back in her chair again, raising her blanket to her collarbone. At a time when she was supposed to be mentally free to focus one hundred and ten percent on her new business, she felt like her mind was clouded with distracting thoughts. Thoughts she didn't care to delve into.

"The warehouse couldn't be better. I thanked Mike a million times for the opportunity. The flexible hours were just what I needed. As for me, I guess I'm still just figuring out life, that's all. I thought by now I'd have it all together. Ha! Fat chance. I still have more work to do."

Clara folded her arms, addressing both of them firmly. "What's really going on, you guys? Mack, I never hear you talk about being sad, and Agnes, I could've sworn you'd be through the roof about getting back to focusing on the food truck. Talk to me. Mack, you first, and then Agnes."

The sound of night crickets and water echoed in the background. The conversation shifted more into a therapy session, with Clara as the lead therapist. But she was okay with it, knowing ultimately Clara really cared.

Mackenzie cleared her throat. "I don't know what to say, ladies. I'm a momaholic first and a workaholic second. The only problem is, I feel like I failed Stephanie miserably by not marrying a man that would be there for her, and I'm out of work right now. From where I sit, it feels like everything is collapsing all at once. The only thing good that came out of the week was the interview about the café. Other than that —" Mack groaned.

Agnes probed, trying to stay in the loop. "What happened with Stephanie?"

"The kids are teasing her at school about not having a father who's present. I'd like to wring their little necks, but we all know that's not the answer. It's just an emotional reaction."

"Man, I feel sorry for her," Clara said.

"Yeah, I do too, but at least she has one friend who is super sweet. Marissa is her name. She's at her house now. I promised I'd let them hang out for a couple of hours." Her voice drifted, not sounding like the usual energetic personality that she normally was.

"You know it's not your fault that her dad is absent in her life, right? If it were up to you, things would be different... much different," Clara said.

"I know."

"I hope you do. I also hope you can see there's another wonderful man in the picture now, a husband in the making, if you ask me."

"Yeah, about that. Brody is truly amazing, but I really don't see why he'd want to commit to somebody like me. You'd think he'd go after a woman with far fewer problems," Mack replied.

Clara admonished her for thinking such thoughts. "You really need to get back to work. Keep it up and I'm going to call Mike and ask him to find a position for you as well. Something to keep your mind busy until the café is ready to reopen." She teased.

"I probably need it. But seriously, it feels good to say these things out loud. Even if there isn't a thing I can do about it with Stephanie or the café. It at least feels good to talk to someone."

The ladies nodded in agreement, then settled, refocusing their attention on Agnes.

"What about you, Miss Agnes? What kind of secrets have you been keeping to yourself these days?" Clara asked with a sly grin plastered across her face.

"Sorry. I wish I had something for ya. Just trying to figure things out, as I mentioned earlier. Living a mundane life, I suppose."

Mack piped her voice up, singing to her. "That's not what I heard."

"What do you mean?"

"My sources tell me that someone was spotted on the island spending quality time with the handsome author," she replied.

"Oh, that was nothing. Mere casual conversation in passing," Agnes said, waving it off.

"Conversation that involved you locking lips?" Mackenzie said.

Clara piped up. "Oh, that's old news. Even I knew about them kissing. Agnes, I knew that would come back to bite you in the rear end. I just didn't want to say anything," Clara replied.

Mack jumped in, defending Agnes. "How could she avoid it? My source tells me she saw them walking to the car at Stoney Point last night, and before Agnes could see what was coming, he was all over her." Mack sniggled. "My source also said they could tell by your response that you didn't seem too upset about it."

Agnes bounced out of her chair like a jack-in-the-box, immediately folding her blanket so she could make a departure.

"Oh, no, you don't. It sounds like you have some explaining to do. Is this true?" Clara asked, poking a little fun, enjoying the gossip just as much as Mackenzie.

Agnes pinched her fingers together. "There may be a wee bit of truth to it. But, it doesn't matter. I woke up this morning, thought about it, and I'm never seeing him again. So, that solves that."

Agnes knew herself all too well to continue hanging out with Grant. If she once questioned her level of attraction toward the handsome writer, last night's kiss sealed the deal, solidifying all of her suspicions. She went all in with her response to his kiss. He was into her, and man, oh man, was she into him.

"Wait. Can you rewind this whole thing from the top, please? Clearly my head has been buried in the sand, missing out on all the tea," Clara said.

"Trust me. You're not missing out on anything. We agreed to hang out sometimes. I thought we could handle it as friends. Clearly, I was wrong. That's it. End of story. Oh, and if it helps to satisfy your curiosity, he's a romance writer." She began walking away before turning around to add one last thought. "And he's a pretty darn good kisser while we're at it. Try to keep the genre between us. I'd ask you to do the same about the kiss, but apparently Solomons Island already knows all about it."

Agnes waved as she exited the deck, stirring up a healthy dose of innocent frustration for Clara. "You're breaking the rules of girl time, Agnes. You can't just get up and leave when the conversation is about you," she said.

With an instinct for needing to have the last word, Agnes yelled from the kitchen. "If I come back out there, the only topic I want to hear about is your secret plan to elope!" she said, then cackled to herself.

Mae Middleton placed her toothbrush back in the holder, applied her lipstick, and gave herself the once over before turning off the bathroom lights. She had a full day of tours lined up, each of them focused on the local lighthouse, while Jonathan, on the other hand, planned to stay home, enjoying a day off.

She stepped into the hall, noticing him dozing comfortably in his recliner. With his mouth cocked open, she hesitated to wake him, thinking it might be best to leave a note on the coffee table.

The ringing sound of the doorbell interrupted her plans and startled him out of his sleep.

"I'll get the door," she said.

Through the side panel, she saw the rear frame of a woman looking around the front yard.

*She won't quit to save her life.* She mumbled to herself.

"Who won't quit?" Jonathan asked. But it was too late. Mae was already unlatching the first and second lock, feverishly trying to open the door.

Meredith, their neighbor, whipped around, graciously greeting her on the other side of the threshold.

"Good morning, Mae. I'm so glad I caught you guys before you left for work." She smiled, handing her a flier.

"Oh. Hi, Meredith."

Jonathan approached the door, giving Mae a look. She knew instinctively what he was thinking but chose not to indulge him.

"Well, hello to you too. Don't worry, I won't keep you long. I just stopped by to tell you about our next meeting coming up. It's going to be a biggy. The homeowners will vote on making a few amendments to our budget, so your presence is definitely needed," she said, sounding proud to be the HOA president.

"Meredith, I'll have to check my work schedule for the upcoming week, but thanks for letting us know." Mae gave her a closed-mouth smile, knowing full well she hated attending those darn meetings in the first place. Sitting there listening to a bunch of folks argue or simply listening to the ones who love to be in front of the microphone was not her cup of tea. Never had been.

"Is that all? I hate to be in such a rush, but I have to get to work."

"Certainly. I'll let you get to it. Have a great day!" She waved, giving them an extra wink and Mae closed the door behind her.

"That woman takes her role way too seriously. Since when did the board start going around door-to-door to announce meetings? Heck, I can vote by proxy and get the minutes in the mail." She grumbled, then headed to the kitchen to grab a quick bottle of water.

Jonathan followed her. "The woman is just doing her job, Mae. Be nice. After all, we voted for her as the HOA president. What I'd like to know is what did you mean by that comment you made about —" but before he could finish, he was cut off by the sound of the doorbell ringing again.

This time it prompted Mae to fuss, marching all the way back down the hall with her purse and bottle of water in hand.

"Good grief. If she comes back here with one more announcement about the HOA, I swear I'm going to —"

Mae swung the door open, only to see Edith standing on the other side.

Edith offered a big smile, extending her hand. "Eh em. Hello. You must be Mae. I'm Edith, your new neighbor."

"Edith. Yes. Nice to meet you. I've heard so much about you," Mae replied, leaving Edith's hand suspended in the air. "To what do we owe the pleasure?"

Mae felt Jonathan brush up against her. It was his subtle way of begging her to behave herself, but she wasn't sure she felt like taking the bait.

"Oh, hi, Jonathan." Edith perked up at his appearance. "My apologies. I promised myself I wouldn't disturb you again unless I had a real problem. I even called the handyman's emergency hotline, but he's stuck at another job."

"What's the problem, Edith?" he asked.

Mae could feel her skin turning various shades of red. *The audacity*, she thought.

The more she watched the woman, the more she could see how Jonathan could easily get roped in, especially given that he was so mild-mannered.

Edith continued. "It's the dish disposal you installed. Whenever I use it, there's a rattling sound that won't quit."

Mae's lips parted as she spoke, but Jonathan intervened.

"Edith, while it may be a little frustrating, I definitely think it's safe. I'll tell you what. Since I'm the one who installed it, I'll come and take a look. How about I stop by this evening around —"

*He can't be serious*, Mae thought to herself, huffing and feeling anxious.

"Six o'clock maybe? That way, Mae can join me. It will be the perfect time for you two to get to know one another and get caught up on all the ins and outs of Solomons Island."

Edith's bright smile slowly drooped, leaving Mae feeling a lot more satisfied.

"That's a wonderful idea, honey. I'll bet Edith would love the inside scoop on the good eateries in town and recommendations for the best salons."

"Oh, I do my hair and nails. Especially now that I'm a homeowner. I have to save where I can," she replied.

"Well, either way, it will be fun getting to know one another while Jonathan looks at your disposal. As long as six o'clock works for you?" Mae asked.

"Um, sure. I don't see why not. I'll see you at six."

"Wonderful." Mae watched her leave, then drew the door closed. She was guaranteed to be late by this point, but acknowledging what Jonathan did for her was far more important.

Before she could speak, he gently tugged at her waistline, bringing them closer until she could feel the warmth coming from his body. He glided his lips softly over hers. "I'm sorry for what I said the other day. I was wrong, and you were right," he whispered.

"Oh, boy. You are something else, Jonathan Middleton. It's the perfect one liner to give a woman when you want to get back in her good graces." She chuckled.

He smiled. "Is it working?"

"You bet it is."

He slid his hand along her back, holding her even closer.

"You know I'd never do anything to compromise what we have, right?" he asked.

"I know you wouldn't, honey. I was acting childish, I'll admit. And who knows? Maybe there's a healthy jealous streak in me. Either way, it never hurts to keep an eye out for women who try to befriend my husband," she said, kissing him back as tenderly as she knew how.

"Keep that up and you will not make it to work at all, Anna Mae." He laughed. "Later on, when we finish at Edith's, I'm planning something special for you."

"Really?" she asked.

"Yes, my love. An evening for two."

This time she eased her lips over his, stirring up heat between them. She'd hoped to give him just enough to miss her until she returned.

# CHAPTER 9

"Welcome to Warehouse Storage. How may I help you?" Agnes whipped around whimsically, stunned to see Clara standing at the front door.

"Hey, Clara. Didn't expect to see you here so bright and early. Actually, what are you doing here? Aren't you normally opening up for Lighthouse Tours by now?" she asked, glancing at the clock.

"Usually, but Mike has everything under control. I thought I'd come down here and check on my baby sis. You know, to see how things are going," she said, looking at her mysteriously.

"Everything is great. I already told you about the job last night, silly. Things couldn't be better. Brody is showing the new guy around this afternoon, so that should be fun, and —"

"Hmm."

Agnes paused, recognizing the sound of uncertainty in Clara's voice. "Okay, talk to me. What's the real reason you stopped by? And spare me the baloney in advance, Clara. Might as well cut right to the chase."

The distance that was once between them after years of being apart had completely dissipated.

Clara dove in. "Fine. Why won't you call him back, for starters?"

"Who?"

"Don't play dumb, Agnes. The author. Did he do something to warrant you not calling him back? I let it go last night, watching you quickly disappear down to the basement, trying to avoid the topic altogether. But I'm not letting you avoid the question now," she said.

"Okay, I'll start right after you tell me more about your new wedding plans. What's this about plans for a honeymoon in Hawaii around the first of the month?"

"Agnes, who told you about Hawaii?" Clara asked.

"I can tell you who didn't tell me."

Clara stood with her eyebrows tied in knots, which prompted Agnes to show a little grace.

"Fine. I accidentally overheard someone leaving a message on your answering machine from the hotel. Not that it was any of my business. It just would've been nice for you to give me the heads up. If you're even the least bit curious to know how I feel about it, I completely support whatever you and Mike decide to do." Agnes' voice trailed off, leaving the atmosphere feeling rather somber.

"I appreciate the support, Ag. But Mike and I have been talking it over. I'll confess that we were this close to completely eloping. Instead, we're flying his parents here early and having a small ceremony on the island. Then, we're taking off for an early honeymoon at the beginning of next month. I was just waiting for confirmation from the hotel, and then we were to sit down with you, collectively, and share. We don't want to wait any longer to be married. And yes, we're making a lot of changes, but not to the extent that I would exclude you."

Agnes spread her arms wide open, approaching her sister with an apologetic smile.

"Does this mean I still get to be in your wedding?" she asked.

"Yes. I can't get married without my maid of honor. There's no way."

Agnes smiled even bigger than before. "Good. Looks like we have some work to do."

"Not really. All the hard work is done. Outside of calling the bakery, booking the restaurant for a small dinner afterward, oh and going in for one last fitting," Clara said.

Thankfully, Agnes knew better. "Don't forget to reschedule your hair appointment."

"Oooh, how could I forget about my hair?" Clara asked.

"Mm hmm. And to think you were about to do this without me." Agnes teased.

"Okay. So, maybe I need some help going over my to-do list later on. But, in the meantime, you still didn't answer my question. Why aren't you calling the author back?"

Agnes wandered around a bit with her arms resting comfortably under her chest.

"I'm not getting involved with anyone. Especially not someone like him. There's no way I'm ever going to put myself in a position to become so vulnerable the way I did with —" Again her voice trailed off, this time realizing she was saying too much. It had been a long while since she and Clara had a conversation about her past with Keith. Let's be honest, it wasn't easy talking to her sister about dating her ex-husband. A man they both had personal encounters with at different points in their lives.

"Go ahead. Finish your sentence. I've long moved on from the likes of somebody like Keith. It doesn't bother me to hear you talk about him, Agnes."

"Really?" she asked.

Clara raised her ring finger before her. Not taunting her, but as a reminder. "I'm about to marry the man of my dreams. Nobody has time for Keith, or for allowing negative experiences from the past to ruin the present and the future. It's a lesson I was hoping you would've learned by now, but I see you haven't caught on just yet."

"Ouch," Agnes responded.

"Sorry, sis. But it's coming from a place of love."

Agnes exhaled.

"I don't disagree with you. But what's wrong with me taking time to myself, anyway? That's what the sabbatical was supposed to be about. I don't need a man to be happy. If I never get married, it would probably be the wisest choice I've ever made. I haven't exactly scored aces with my choice in men. Even prior to Keith, the options weren't looking too good." She chuckled, tucking her hair behind her ears. She knew if they stood there long enough, Clara would share the kind of wisdom they used to get from their mother before she passed away. A part of her desired the reassurance.

"Again. What does your past have to do with anything? It's the decisions you make today that will influence your tomorrow, Ag. Let me tell you something. It's very possible that your sabbatical has an expiration date. Perhaps it's already expired. But you'll never know if you go around hiding from men for the rest of your life. Is the author guy nice?"

Agnes' closed-mouth smile spoke volumes. "He is. I actually like talking to him. We appear to have a lot in common."

"What's the big deal with continuing to get to know him while he's here?" Clara asked.

"Because he'll be leaving before you know it. That's the big deal. I don't want to start falling for someone and then watch him pack his bags and leave. I'm definitely not subjecting myself to a long distance relationship — so there — Now you can see why I won't be calling him anymore. Not even to hang out as so-called friends."

Just then, a customer pushed through the door with his wife and two kids in tow. Agnes put on a customer friendly smile, choosing to act as if their conversation never took place.

"Welcome to Lighthouse Storage. How can I help you?" she asked, promptly leaving her sister behind and grateful for the interruption.

Later that evening Brody assisted Mack in the kitchen, clearing the dishes from a meal he prepared for three. Stephanie was in her room, entertaining herself on the computer, leaving the two of them to talk about the events of the day.

"Brody, you're spoiling me and Stephanie. Coming over here after a hard day's work to prepare us dinner. That's really going above and beyond," she said.

He chuckled. "I'd hardly call chicken parmesan and spaghetti a form of spoiling anybody."

"I beg to differ. The meal was delicious, and the proof was Steph asked for seconds. The only thing she ever asks me for is to be excused from the table. I guess I'm no Brody or Chef Harold."

He hoisted her up by the waist, gently placing her on the countertop.

"And God knows I'm grateful for it. If you were Chef Harold, I wouldn't be able to snuggle up close to you like I am right now." Brody softly nuzzled against her neck, inhaling her scent, causing her to relax. She loved how strong he was and how much of a good man he was on the inside.

Mack lowered her voice. "Brody, you are so bad. If

Stephanie walks in here and sees us all over each other, what is she going to think?" she asked, all the while drawing him in even closer, reciprocating with flirtatious gestures.

He brought his lips up to her ear. "Okay, one quick kiss, and then I'll let you go."

"How about you make it two quick kisses? Then, I'll let you go." She teased, keeping her

legs locked around Brody's, allowing him to give her more like four or five kisses, before pulling herself together, turning down the heat for the sake of her daughter, Stephanie.

He lifted her, gently letting her down to the floor, exchanging one last peck before returning to drying the dishes.

"I have good news for you," she said.

He smiled. "I'm all ears."

"I heard from the reporter today. Looks like they're going to release the article right after the reopening. She thought if we timed it right, it might help shine a little light on the café, hopefully drawing in a sizeable crowd."

"Mack, that's wonderful. See, I told you everything would fall in place as it should. Even the schedule with the contractors is going smoothly, and these days, that's practically unheard of," he replied.

"Thanks, love. I'm feeling better about it. Guess I just needed a day or two to get myself together. I spoke to Beth from the store next door. She seems to be holding it together as well, even though her store suffered a lot more damage and will take a little longer to re-open."

He took the last dish out of her hand and began drying it. "You both will be fine. It will be a new beginning. A fresh start allowing both businesses to come out even stronger than before. Mark my words, this time next year, you'll be able to look back and be amazed at all you've accomplished."

She laughed. "Brody, I'll tell ya. They aren't making men

like you anymore. I think you're still one of the last few wandering this earth."

"Hey, I'm just calling it like I see it. You're going to make a strong comeback. You and the staff will be just fine," he said.

"I sure hope so. When I spoke to Joshua, he seemed rather happy to have the extra time to work on his auto parts business, and Dakota just seems restless. The same with Chef Harold. I'm hoping they won't apply for jobs elsewhere. If they do—"

"Mackenzieeee. If you don't stop torturing yourself with all the what ifs, I'm going to put you right back on that counter again." He flirted.

"Okay, okay. I'll behave."

"Thank you. Now, it's my turn to share some good news with you," he said.

"Please do. I need all the good news I can get."

Brody leaned on the counter next to Mack. "I spoke to my dad while you were with the girls last night. He asked about you and me. He was wondering how things were progressing and if I thought you were the one."

Mack's mouth fell open. "He said that to you?"

"Yes, he sure did. And you know what? For once in my life, I had no hesitation in my response. The answer came naturally to me, just like being here with you is natural."

She held down her head, trying not to expose her broad smile. "What did you say to him?"

"You certain you want to know?" he asked.

"Yes."

Brody folded the dish towel and hung it over the rack. "I told him I'm going to ask you to marry me someday. I also told him it won't be long before I do it. Of course, it's important to me to have this conversation with Stephanie first. But, as long as she approves, I'm going for it with everything that I've got.

You're the one for me, Mack. There's no question in my mind about it."

"I'm speechless," she said.

"Is that a good sign?"

"It's not a bad thing by any means. It just feels like somebody turned the thermostat way up high." She smiled, fanning herself. Brody's words were turning up the heat in her veins in a good way. The only thing she hoped for was a clear conscious. One freed from all the other things that were currently cluttering her mind.

"I guess this is a good time for me to share something about Steph. You know she views you as a father figure, right? It comes naturally, as we all spend more time together."

He lifted her hand and placed it in the palm of his. "I've noticed, and you need to know that it's something I don't take for granted."

"I know you don't. It's just — The kids at school. They've been giving her a hard time about it, and I'm trying to support her as best as I can. I've even reached out to her teacher, but there's only so much I can do. It angers me that her father is not present in her life, and it frustrates me that I can't be everything she needs." Her voice tapered off while she wiped tears from her eyes.

"Are you kidding me? You have been an amazing parent to Steph. I think you're being way too hard on yourself," he said. Then, he gripped her by the shoulders, meeting her eye-to-eye. "Perhaps you're going through a small rough patch, feeling sad about everything collectively. But, I'll bet if you were to ask Steph her thoughts about you as a mother, there would be nothing but high praises."

She chuckled while dabbing her eyelids. "I don't know about that. Let it be a day where I say no to sweets, and I'm certain those praises would turn into resentment."

"Okay, I think you get a free pass on trying to spare the kid from having stomach aches and dental issues. Trust me, as she gets older, she'll understand."

"I sure hope so. Not just about the sweets, but about everything."

Brody placed Mackenzie's head on his shoulder. She closed her eyes, feeling appreciative of the comfort and the safety he provided.

"Mack, I don't know what it's like to be a father. I have absolutely no idea. But I know the example of a father's love. I know what it feels like to have someone love me uncondition-ally and take care of me. If you decide to ever trust me with that responsibility someday, I promise I'll pass that same level of love on to her. You can count on it."

She tilted her head upward. "I already do trust you, Brody. I already do."

~

Mae crossed the threshold of Edith's door with a tray of cookies in hand. They were nicely covered with saran wrap and a big yellow bow with a welcome card attached.

"Edith, this is for you," she said, proudly presenting the baked goods.

Jonathan also greeted her and then asked permission to head to the kitchen. With his tool bag in hand, he left the ladies to talk.

"Mae, how nice of you. Home-baked cookies to welcome me to the neighborhood. Boy, did I choose the right place to live, or what?" She smiled. Mae wasn't sure she could trust the woman further than her eyes could see her, but if she was going to find a balance between keeping the peace and protecting what was hers, she figured this was a good start.

"I'll confess that I didn't bake them from scratch. They came from Solomons Bakery. Just about a mile north of here. If you have a sweet tooth, or just a craving for freshly baked desserts, you'll definitely want to stop by. Tell Mel I sent you. That way, she'll give you her Tuesday afternoon discount." She placed the tray on Edith's dining table, then offered her undivided attention.

"So, Jonathan shared with me you're from Annapolis."

Edith glanced toward the kitchen. "Yes, I am. Looks like we have that in common. Can I offer you something to drink?" she asked.

"No, thank you. I hope you don't mind me coming over with Jonathan, but I figured as many times as he's been here, it was time for me to come and introduce myself."

In the background, Mae could hear Jonathan coughing loudly, or at least pretending to do so to get her attention.

"Are you all right, dear?" she said, perching her ear up.

"I'm fine. Just tightening a loose screw," he yelled back.

Edith continued. "Yes, I suppose I owe you an apology. Ever since I moved into this place, it's been one thing or another. Of course, it's no excuse. I should've been able to detect some of these issues with my inspector, not Jonathan."

"Inspectors can't detect everything. Some things you have to figure out as you go. I'm just glad Jonathan could connect you with some of the guys down at the hardware store. Also, I'd be happy to introduce you to Meredith, our HOA president. I'm sure she has a plethora of resources right at her fingertips." Mae laughed and leaned a little closer. "Everybody likes to refer to her as the town mayor. She definitely has a knack for knowing everything that's going on in the community. Outside of that, she's a wonderful woman... very resourceful. I'll have to introduce you. I'm sure she'd be glad to take you under her wing."

Jonathan reappeared, clearing his throat.

"Edith, I think you're all set. It was a simple oversight on my part. I was probably in such a hurry that somehow I left a screw loose. You shouldn't have any more trouble out of your brand new disposal from here on out."

Mae observed as Edith respectfully thanked Jonathan, not overstepping any boundaries, as she once suspected. That alone made her feel good about the decision to come introduce herself. *Sometimes the presence of your significant other makes all the difference,* she thought to herself.

"Mae, thanks again for the cookies. I can't wait to dig in," Edith said.

"It was my pleasure. Nice meeting you."

Mae and Jonathan said their goodbyes, and by the time they made it to the curbside, he was already teasing his wife, chuckling uncontrollably at her.

"Jonathan, dare I ask what's so funny? I thought I was neighborly and very well behaved." She suggested.

"Oh, you were on your best behavior, all right. What did you say again? 'I figured with as many times as he's been over, it was time for me to come and introduce myself.' Mae, that was terrible. Do you really think she couldn't read between the lines?" he asked, shaking his head.

Mae didn't see the humor in it, but Jonathan was sweet about it, tugging her closer, placing his arm around her neck.

"It's okay, my love. I've never seen this protective, maybe even a little jealous, side of you, but I'll tell you one thing. I like it," he said, kissing her temple.

"Oh, Jonathan." She grumbled.

"Anna Mae. You can't explain yourself out of this one if you tried. All I want to know is, do you feel better about the whole thing now that you've met her?"

"Yes, I do. As long as she respects our boundaries, calling

on the handymen, instead of you. On another note, don't think that I didn't hear you coughing in the kitchen, Jonathan. I knew what you were up to," she said, poking at him.

If she was being honest, she knew the best approach would be to trust Jonathan to handle it going forward. She knew he would do the right thing, as he'd been doing all along.

When they reached their driveway, she stopped him. "I owe you an apology, Jonathan. I took on an accusatory tone with you in the garage the other day. Even though it didn't help to hear you refer to Edith as beautiful, I know it was an innocent mistake."

"One that I completely regret. I'm the one who's sorry. Mae, you know that I only have eyes for you, right?" Jonathan asked.

"I do. But, say it again, and I promise —" Mae playfully balled up her fists, but before she could follow through with her threat, Jonathan picked her up, tossing her over his shoulder to head inside and enjoy an evening at home for two.

# CHAPTER 10

*A*gnes Covington skimmed the dessert case as she had done several times a week. With the closing of the café, the coffee shop had become one of her favorite places to work on her off days as she finalized her plans for the food truck. Harvey prepared her usual latte, and all that was left to do was decide between the strudel and a danish. Not such a difficult task, but yet an enormous deal every single time.

"Shoot," she whispered, noticing Grant crossing the street, coming toward the shop. *I can't catch a break with this guy.*

"Harvey, I need a quick favor. Let's hold off on the dessert for a minute. Instead, I was wondering if you'd let me go to the back and hide for a while until the author guy leaves?" She begged.

Harvey caught a glimpse of him approaching the store as well and smiled.

"What, are we in high school? Sorry, no can do. It's against store policy to allow customers in the employee section."

She rolled her eyes. "Harvey, it's me we're talking about

here. Nobody has to know. Come on, I'm sure he'll be in and out of here. Less than five minutes, tops."

"Again, I'm sorry. I have to play by the rules. Besides, it's already too late. He's coming in as we speak. I'm not sure what you have against the guy, but he's good looking, has a distinguished career, and he clearly likes you. A lot. Here's a thought. Instead of running away from him, why don't you try getting to know the guy? Practically the entire time he's been staying here, all he ever does is ask about you."

"Wait. What?" she asked.

Harvey motioned his head toward Grant, who was now standing behind her.

"Grant. How are you?" she said, trying to seem surprised to see him. "Fancy meeting you here."

"I just dropped in to grab a cup to go. You can relax. I have no intention of bothering you or trying to strike up a conversation, if that's what you're worried about," he replied.

"Oh. Well, I wasn't assuming anything. I was just saying hello."

She watched as he put in an order for his favorite coffee, then grabbed a napkin and waited patiently along the side, letting other customers go. Somehow, she'd completely forgotten about placing her own order and was now intrigued as to why he wasn't pursuing her, as he'd done so many times before.

"Harvey, when you get a chance, can you wrap up a danish to go?" she asked.

"I thought you were hanging out for a while?" Harvey continually darted his eyes toward Grant to no avail. Then, once he saw his efforts weren't getting anywhere, he lost his cool and intervened. "That does it. I've had it with you two. This charade has gone on long enough. Of all the things I've witnessed from behind this counter, this little thing the two of you have going on is by far the most aggravating to date. So, for the record, I'm just going to come right out and tell the truth," he said.

On the side lines Agnes could see Grant mouthing something to Harvey, but it was too late. Harvey looked as if he was over it.

"It's all my fault. I guess you can blame me for overstepping my boundaries and getting involved. I should've exercised some good sense and stayed out of it, but I've always been a sucker for love. Agnes Covington, this man is smitten over you. From the moment he laid eyes on you, all he's ever wanted was an opportunity to meet you." Harvey continued.

By this point, she noticed Grant practically squirming, turning beat red, obviously not expecting Harvey to divulge his secrets.

"I innocently may have shared your usual times for visiting the coffee shop. Heck, he was suffering from writer's block, and you needed something to do besides worrying about your business endeavors all the time. I thought it was a good idea at the onset. However, you two are the most stubborn individuals I have ever met," Harvey said, frowning at Agnes and then Grant.

"Hey, don't look at me. She's the one who won't take my calls. I'm assuming I offended her in some kind of way. Even though, if that's the case, I still don't know what I did. It doesn't matter, anyway. We should all just drop it. I know how to take a hint," Grant replied.

Thankful the shop was rather quiet, mostly, the random one or two customers that came in and placed orders, listened until their items were paid for and left.

"You did nothing wrong," she whispered.

Harvey and Grant both looked at her with an expression that spoke volumes.

"Well, then, why haven't you been taking my calls?" he asked.

When she didn't respond, he politely thanked Harvey for his help, grabbed his cup, and proceeded to leave.

Harvey slid her cup across the counter, then pointed toward the front door. "He's one of the good ones, Agnes."

"How do you know?"

"I spend seven days a week listening to people sit around here, sharing their life stories. I know everything about his family back home, his writing career, and I know that he, like yourself, has been hurt before but is willing to take a chance on love. I think I'm qualified," Harvey responded.

"How do you know that I've been hurt before? I never told you that."

"It's written all over your face. You're just as guarded as they come. Plus, he told me about your sabbatical. Honey, please. I see the way you look at that man." He laughed.

She leaned in. "Did he tell you about the kiss?"

"Which one?"

"Great, you must know everything at this point," she said.

"I'll tell you what I don't know. I don't understand why you're not going after him. Go. Get out of here already."

"Harvey, he's about to leave. What difference will any of this make after he's gone?"

"Listen to me, kiddo. It may make all the difference in the world. But you'll never know if you don't go after him. I'd take my chances if I were you. It beats being alone."

Harvey passed her a complementary danish to go with her coffee.

"Go get him, tiger." He smiled.

≈

"Grant, wait. Grant," Agnes yelled. She spotted the back of his jacket walking at a fast pace along the boardwalk.

"Grant." She cried out one last time, nearly breathless, and fighting the urge to fuss at him.

"Agnes?" he said, turning around.

"Hey, I was calling your name all the way down the boardwalk."

He removed one of his ear buds, waving it in front of her.

"Kind of hard to hear when you have music playing. I was trying to get into a creative zone before heading back to the house."

"Ear buds, of course. That makes sense."

She knew the awkward moment called for an explanation but was struggling to work up the nerve to say what was really on her mind.

"Did you want something?" he asked.

"No. Yes. The answer is yes. I came out here to say I'm sorry."

"There's no need. Really. The more I think about it, the more I realize I'm the one at fault here. I was laying it on way too thick. We were supposed to be hanging out as friends and I let my feelings get the best of me. I was probably living in my world of fiction more than reality," he replied.

"What's that supposed to mean?"

He chuckled. "Underneath this exterior lies the heart of a hopeless romantic, wishing that one day he could stop hiding behind his keyboard and actually get out there and meet some-one. I'm a loner, Agnes. By choice, I spend my days creating fictitious stories, hoping to inspire people to believe in love. When the book is complete, I write the words, the end, and then return to my lonely reality. It's the story of my life, or at least it was until the day we met. You captivated my attention... I even started looking forward to running into you."

"What's so special about me, Grant? If only you'd been around the day I showed up with my bags from New York. I was a hot mess back then and I still am. I'll bet money you wouldn't have the same opinion of me if you really knew what I was all about." Her eyes drifted over to the water in shame, then back over to him, waiting for a response.

"I don't know what to say," Grant replied.

"Exactly."

"Agnes, let me finish my thought. I don't know what to say regarding who you were and what brought you here. All I know is I'm interested in getting to know the woman standing in front of me now. And, the sad part is, time is running out. If you're not interested in return, I understand. Now, respectfully. I have to get back to work. I have a deadline to meet."

He wedged his ear buds back in place and waved goodbye.

"Grant, wait." She called out.

He stopped.

"The thing is, I'm into you too. I have been ever since the day I spilled coffee on you. Always thought you were good looking. And you're definitely a good kisser." She teased.

He pointed to himself. "Who me?" he said, looking around.

It was little moments like those that caused her to find him so irresistible. She loved his dimples, and even more so, she loved how candid he was about his feelings. But how could she freely explore where things could lead with his impending departure? *It wouldn't make any sense,* she thought.

"Grant, now that we've been transparent with one another, there's only one problem."

He wouldn't hear of it. Instead, he placed his finger over her lips.

"Shh. Don't do it. Don't dwell on the many ways this can go wrong. Instead, just enjoy the moment with me. Please?" He pleaded.

She could hear the intensified sound of her heart beating out of control.

"But —"

"Agnessssss,"

"Yes," she whispered.

Grant came within inches of her lips, but he didn't kiss her.

"Let's allow ourselves the pleasure of enjoying what today brings, and let tomorrow take care of itself. Meet me at my place tonight around seven. I'll text you the address."

"Okay," she responded with her eyes closed, leaning in anticipation of a kiss.

By the time she looked again, his lips were kissing her hand ever so gently, sending a strong current through her body.

His beach rental was contemporary, with clean lines resting just a stone's throw away from the sand leading to the water. His neighbors also had contemporary shaped beach houses with private views and boat slips in the backyard. It was the kind of place she'd only dreamed about living in. *This is perfect for a writer*, Agnes thought as she imagined him using the beach as a backdrop or a makeshift office.

She mashed the bell, hoping not to look ridiculous while being recorded on the doorbell camera. Within a moment's time, she could see him coming down the hall.

"Hey there," he answered.

"I made it."

"You did, and you're right on time. Please come in. Welcome to my temporary home." He admitted. He passed her a bouquet of orchids, mixed with an assortment of wildflowers, vibrant, just like the art on the wall and the decor.

Grant stood about six feet tall, wearing a white polo with

jeans. His beard was cut to precision, giving him just enough of that rugged look she liked, but not totally bare and clean shaven. Being handsome came naturally to him, but the most attractive part was he didn't even seem to know it.

"Thanks for inviting me here tonight. I have to admit that I've never been to an author's place before. It makes me feel kind of special getting a behind the scenes look at the hopeless romantic's humble abode... perhaps in this case, not so humble, as this place is absolutely massive." She teased.

He paid special attention to her smile and then proceeded to explain.

"Yeah, you're right. It's big, but it's the views for me. I used to dream about having a writing space with a picturesque view. Plus, the owner worked out a month-to-month agreement with me that was rather sweet. So, I can't complain. Would you like a tour?" he asked.

"Sure."

She followed him around the main floor, touring the music room, guest accommodations, outdoor access to a private pool, the kitchen, and finally landed in a room he set aside especially for writing.

"This is it. This is my main space for creativity. It's a bit of a mess, as you can see, but this is how I produce my best work."

Agnes took a slow tour of the room, noticing a huge glass window overlooking the Patuxent with sliding glass doors. The walls were labeled with notes taped around the perimeter of the room for various chapters of his book. Character profiles, names of places, and important events that would take place.

"It looks like organized chaos. A little of this, tons of notes, a little of that, oh and a lot of drawings.

"Are you an artist too?" she asked.

He chuckled. "I wish. That's just my way of fleshing out my characters. Some people like to hunt for random pictures on the internet to use as visuals for their characters. I like to draw mine. It's like having a therapeutic creativity session. Take this the right way, but sometimes while I'm drawing I can even hear —"

"The characters' voices talking in your head?" She giggled.

"Yes. I rarely admit it. People might start to think I'm loco," he said, twirling his finger around his head.

"I wouldn't think that. Many years ago, I signed up for a creative writing course. The instructor talked about hearing the characters' voices in your head. It's totally normal."

Again, she caught him looking at her in admiration.

Grant cleared his throat. "One of my favorite things about living out here is the soothing sound of the water and the tranquility at night. It takes my breath away. Most evenings I can come out here on one of my breaks and see the stars hanging so low, it's as if I can touch them. Sometimes it gets me to thinking about our creator. Other times, it encourages me to dream about the unknown things in life," he said.

"Like?"

"It's hard to explain, but sometimes I like to sit out here and contemplate my life and my purpose, and what direction I'm heading in. I mean, I know I'm supposed to be a writer, but I often wonder if there are even greater things that I'm called to do. Living the life of a traveling author and seeing the world has been amazing, but it gets lonely."

He invited her to follow him into the kitchen as they continued to talk.

"What places have you traveled to?" she asked.

"San Francisco, Europe, San Juan, New York, Colorado... gorgeous mountains, by the way. If you haven't been, you really need to visit."

She watched his body language as he continued to describe his various trips, his passion, and his enthusiasm for his work. It made her respect him, perhaps even admire him even more. "I recognize that fire in your eyes. It's the same passion I have for my small business. Of course, it sounds nowhere near as glamorous, but it's special to me just the same."

Grant paused in the middle of laying stir-fry vegetables on the counter.

"Promise me you won't ever do that again," he said.

"What did I do?"

"Belittle your dreams. It's not about how glamorous it sounds or how it compares to my line of work. It's your passion. And, with your creativity, talent, fire, it's going to be the best food truck Solomons Island has ever seen. You got it?" he asked.

"Yes, sir. The absolute best bbq truck ever. They won't know what hit them."

"That's the spirit. Now, while you sit there and watch me make a fool of myself in the kitchen, as I try to impress you, tell me more about Agnes Covington. What do you like to do for fun when you're not planning and working?" He smiled.

"Hmm. That's a good question. I'm not sure I know what fun looks like since moving to the island. Not that it's a dull place to live, by any means. I just came here under crazy circumstances and before you know it, I found myself in the space that I'm in now, planting roots and building a future for myself out here. I think the most fun I've had is probably lying out in my sister's backyard taking in the sun. You sort of caught me at an awkward time."

She watched him pour a splash of olive oil into the pan, and then he made eye contact with her.

"Now, it's all making sense. You ran into me with your coffee that day because you desperately needed to meet a new friend. Someone who would encourage you to pull your head out of the sand and learn how to enjoy life a little." He chuckled.

"Oh, and I guess you're an expert at it. You've got it all figured out, especially as you spend most of the day locked inside the four walls of your beach rental."

Agnes continued to playfully tease, but fully recognized they were living parallel lives, oddly. Both of them needing an escape from their reality, even if it was only for a little while. Her issue was she knew herself all too well. Easily wearing her feelings on her sleeve and falling in love with the wrong men. She didn't want that anymore. It was exhausting, constantly leading her to a dead-end place.

Grant took his flour-coated finger and touched the tip of her nose. "Hold on there, tiger. I never said I had it all figured out. But I do recognize when it's time for change. We're both at a crossroad in our lives with a world of opportunity before us as it pertains to business and work, but... if we're not careful, we might miss out on what matters most. Is that what we really want for ourselves?"

"Did you just put flour on my nose?" she asked.

"Who, me?"

Agnes quickly grabbed a pinch of flour, flicking it at him, and then removed herself to the living area as not to get caught in a war.

Grant revealed all of his pearly whites, appearing to be having a good time. "Ah, there's your playful side coming out. I love it." He laughed.

"Ha ha, funny guy."

She once again noticed additional maps pinned on the walls of various places he'd traveled. "Out of all the places you've visited, I'm surprised you never met someone to settle down with before now. A guy like yourself, in your early forties, a great career, single, without someone to call your own. It doesn't add up."

"I'd have to agree with you. It doesn't add up. Sometimes

we go through things in life that simply fall into alignment with our plans. I wasn't supposed to be a loner. She was supposed to show up at the chapel on time, as planned. We were supposed to exchange our vows and live life happily ever after. The morning came, I got dressed in my tux, and I stood waiting at the altar. She got cold feet and never showed. So, kind of like you said, some things just don't add up."

"I'm sorry, Grant. I didn't realize —"

"Don't be. It's been six years since that event occurred. She's married now. As for me, well, I dove into my writing, finding other ways to create my love story and my happily ever afters."

She felt awful for bringing it up, yet safe, knowing he understood the pain associated with trusting someone who would ultimately let you down.

# CHAPTER 11

*a* month later... Mackenzie flipped the sign on her front door to show the café was open about an hour earlier than usual. At six-thirty a.m. the sun was just coming up, but she didn't care. It had been a long six weeks, with renovations extending beyond the deadline. She was nervous, ready to get back to work, and anxiously waiting to see if some of her regulars would return to the café.

"Joshua, thank you for coming in early. I'm just a ball of nerves these days. I can't eat, can't sleep. My poor daughter probably thinks I'm losing my mind."

"Mack, I just heard her in the back, talking to Harold. She seems fine. It's difficult being out of work for several weeks, I get it. But try to look at the bright side. This grand re-opening is going to do wonders for business. I mean, come on, would you look at this place? Chef Harold is in heaven with all the new appliances, and the little touches you've added to the main floor is giving the café a completely new look. A make-over can do wonders. I'll bet the bridge club and everyone else starts spending double time here, which for you means double the money," he said.

"True. Lord knows we need the extra money. This entire experience taught me a valuable lesson about beefing up my savings account. I have to do better. I can't go down this road again."

"I hear ya. Thankfully, that's all behind us now. I have the side business to sustain me. Dakota's worst complaint was being bored, but she's glad to be coming back. So, it's all good. We're on the upside." He offered.

"Thank you, Joshua. You're just like Brody, always encouraging me when I need it most."

Joshua pointed toward the door. "Speaking of Brody, he's heading across the street now with a ton of balloons in hand. I swear you two were made for each other. All the lovey dovey gestures, for goodness' sake, is enough to make one lose their lunch. I'm going to head to the back and unpack the napkins. That way, you guys can have a moment."

"You're so crazy. Thanks, Joshua." She giggled.

Brody opened the door, carrying two bunches of celebratory balloons. He could hardly fit them through the door, so Mackenzie did her part, helping him, already feeling better about the day.

"Brody, what in the world? How many balloons did you buy?" she asked.

"Enough for you to tie one on the back of each booth and chair. Come on, now. This is a grand reopening. We're celebrating, right?"

"Yes."

"The newspaper is stopping by later this afternoon to get a few candid shots, so I figured, why not? It's just a little something to make it festive and get folks excited about coming back, that's all. Nothing too crazy."

"Wait a minute," she said, sounding serious.

"What? You don't like the balloons? I'm doing too much, aren't I? I'm sorry, I just thought it might be a nice little touch. I didn't think —"

"No, that's not it. I love the balloons. I don't know why I didn't think of it myself. I just told Joshua I'm a ball full of nerves, and all I really need right now, even if it's just for a minute, is to be in your arms, Brody. I just want to thank you, and give you a hug, that's all."

He released the balloons, allowing them to hit the ceiling while grabbing her, pulling her close.

"You don't have to ask me twice. We can hug all day if you'd like. Forget the press. Hugging is my specialty," he said, playfully nibbling on her ear.

"Ha ha, no way, buddy. I love having alone time with you, but I also need to get my business back in order." She smiled.

"And that you shall do. Where's Stephanie?"

"She's in the back, learning a few pointers from Harold before it's time to head to school. If I know right, she's probably chewing his ear off. I think she's just as excited as I am about today. She even says she wants to own a café, just like me when she grows up. Hmm. That will probably change, of course. But it's nice to know I'm doing something right in her eyes."

Her arms fell to her side while he cupped her cheeks in his hands. "Stop being so tough on yourself. You're doing a lot more than you know. Now, what can I do to help you get ready? I don't have to be down to the warehouse until eight. That gives me plenty of time to lend a helping hand."

"I guess you could start by setting up the balloons for me," she said.

"Right. I'm on it. After I'm done, I can even swing Stephanie by her school if you'd like. Only if you're comfortable with me driving her, of course."

"Brody, you're one of the safest drivers I know. Taking Steph would be such a big help, and I know she'd be thrilled to ride in your truck. I'll let her know."

They worked for the next hour straight, refilling the napkin holders, ensuring all the tables had the appropriate condiments, even wiping the chairs down one last time, ensuring that everything was squeaky clean.

"Mom, Chef Harold is teaching me everything I need to know about running the kitchen. He said if it's okay with you, I can come by anytime I want to learn more. Can I stay here instead of going to school today, please?" Stephanie begged.

"Absolutely not. You have a science test coming up soon, and I will not have you miss the review and get a poor grade. Don't you worry. Chef Harold will still be here after school. Now, grab your backpack and make sure you wear your seatbelt while riding with Brody, okay?"

Stephanie hung her head low. "Okay."

Brody whispered to her. "How about you share a few of Chef Harold's tips with me in the truck? I need to get better at cooking for your mom."

She looked up and giggled at him, quickly forgetting about her disappointment.

At the front door Mackenzie could see one of her first customers of the day arriving. She bent down, adjusting Steph's clothing, gave her a kiss, and patted her gently as she joined Brody by his side.

She then approached the gentleman standing at the door. Her heart suddenly skipped a beat, but not in a good way. She felt like she could faint, maybe even be sick, but Mack held her breath and waited. He stood frozen, staring at her, then his eyes drifted over to Steph and Brody, before looking back at her again.

"Ben?" she said.

"Hey, Mackenzie," he responded. The man stood tall, with a rugged beard, ash washed jeans, and boots. He looked like a movie star or a member of a band of some sort. Even had a tattoo crawling up the side of his neck, and a corvette parked out front, which she presumed was his.

"Mommy, who's this man?" Steph asked.

Mack felt herself salivating. "Uh," was all she could say.

"Mackenzie, are you okay?" Brody stepped forward.

"Yeah. Yes, I'm fine. You two need to hurry, so you won't be late for school." She exhaled, peeling her eyes away long enough to reassure Brody that all was well.

Brody protested quietly as not to scare Stephanie. "Are you certain? I'm not getting a good vibe here." He mumbled.

"Brody, I promise, everything is fine. I'll explain more later, but for now, if she misses the bell, they're going to mark her down as tardy."

She put her best smile forward, hoping to put his mind at ease. After another moment of giving the guy the once over, Brody backed off. "Okay, Joshua should be out any minute now. I'll be back."

Mackenzie kissed Stephanie, then watched as they walked out the door.

~

"Babe, can you believe we're getting hitched in a week?" Clara squealed. "I'm so excited I could scream it to the mountain tops," she yelled, flailing her arms in the air.

"Yep, only problem is there's not one mountain in sight. You might want to hold off until we get to Maui for that." Mike teased.

Clara paced around the boat, feeling confident to remain stable without getting seasick. She'd come a long way from their early days of dating, when the thought of sailing would make her want to hurl.

"How does everything look?" she asked, pointing to the setup she prepared for a group of women who booked a three-hour tour to Annapolis and back.

"It looks great. What's not to like? The new boat is stunning. It's an early spring day, and my beautiful bride-to-be is doing an amazing job helping me run the business. Everything is falling in place, and I owe it all to you," he said.

"Mmm. Nope. I'm not taking the credit for what you've done with Lighthouse Tours, Mike. You built this location from the ground up. North Beach as well. Plus, the warehouse, which is coming along nicely, is all because of you."

"And I didn't get any help from my marketing pro?" He smiled.

"Okay, maybe just a little. I'll blame some of that on my grandfather, who used to be a salesman. Maybe he passed down some of his marketing skills in my DNA. But most of this is on you, bud. You're amazing at what you do, and you really need to own it."

"Thank you. I will own it, but right now, I think the idea of leaving this place in someone else's hands for two weeks is starting to settle in," he said.

"Are you feeling nervous about it? You know Brody is totally up for the task. We'll have our seasonal help come over and assist with the tours. Agnes will keep things afloat at the warehouse, and the North Beach office will be just fine," she replied, strapping her arms around his waist.

"I know. It's just my first time taking off for so long. The good news is my parents are going to hang out for at least another week after the ceremony. That way, they can check up on things for me. If nothing else, just being a presence if needed."

"That is wonderful, and don't worry. Everything will be just fine. Now, can we run down our wedding checklist? I promise this version is super quick since the wedding has been reduced to immediate friends and family," she asked.

"Go for it," he said, while hosing the dock area down.

"Okay, let's see. I spoke to Agnes last night. She is picking out a nude pink dress. Something that flows and is easy to wear on the beach. As for Brody, I need you to double check that all is going well with him finding a heather grey suit."

"Heather grey?" Mike asked.

"Yes, it's a lighter shade of grey that will go perfect with Agnes' dress for the pictures. We can't do dark grey. It will throw everything off."

"Heather grey suit for Brody, check." He laughed, shaking his head.

"What's so funny?"

"Nothing, honey. I'm just admiring how precise you are. Keep going," Mike responded, still smiling.

"Mm hmm. Next on the list is the party rental place. I confirmed the chairs, a canopy, a miniature dance floor, oh, and a white arch. Agnes said she'll decorate the arch with flowers the morning of. Then there's the music. I'm at a complete loss for what to do about the music."

"I'm not. Remember the date I planned for you in my back-yard? I had called in a favor for a musician to come and play for us. Why don't I make a few phone calls and see if I can get him back? I'm sure he'd love to perform at our wedding."

Again, she let out a squeal, feeling pleased at the way every-thing was coming together. She knew it would not be a tradi-tional wedding with large crowds of people, but it would be their unique ceremony. That's all that mattered.

"Hey, Mike."

"Yes.

"Thank you for always bending over backward, doing anything you can to take care of me. It doesn't go unnoticed. Not for one second. I love you so much. Always know that."

"Aw, likewise, babe. You mean the world to me, you know that. Besides, I'm only giving you what you deserve."

Clara picked up a push broom and swept the area where Mike hosed.

"Mike. There's something that's been on my mind. Something I realize that you and I never really talk about." She chuckled nervously. "I probably should've brought it up long before now, but somehow it's never been at the forefront of our minds."

He turned off the hose, giving her his undivided attention.

"You know you can talk to me about anything. What's on your mind?" he asked.

She released a deep sigh.

"Do you ever think about adopting a child?"

For what seemed like an entire minute, the only thing Clara could hear was the sound of the waves brushing gently against the boat. Mike inhaled, and then exhaled, torn about the subject.

"It's fine. You don't have to answer that question now. I'm not sure why I brought it up in the first place. I mean, here I am, almost forty-nine years old. Bringing a child into our lives now wouldn't make any sense," she said.

"I completely disagree. I think you'd make a wonderful mother. You're nurturing and kind. Motherhood would come naturally for you. Plus, the idea of giving a child a home, a safe place to grow up, I can't think of a greater sacrifice. Me, on the other hand. I don't know what kind of father I'd be. I rarely have time to practice being an uncle with my very own niece and nephew. They're always traveling the world, heading from one military assignment to the next."

She dropped the broom, embracing him by the shoulders.

"You would be the most amazing dad ever. I know this because of the way you love unconditionally. Mike, you rescued me back when I was afraid for my life. I'll never forget the night you came and stayed with me in my apartment when Joan's family threatened me. You're a protector, a provider, and you make me feel so safe... so loved. That's all a child would ever need. But, to be fair, this is not something we would have to decide overnight. We'll have a lifetime together to think this over. And, if we never adopt, we can just spoil Brody and Mack's kids." She smiled.

"Wait, Mack's pregnant with Brody's baby?"

"No, but it's only a matter of time before those two tie the knot."

"True. I've never seen the guy so smitten. Heck, I don't think I've ever seen him smitten at all." He laughed.

Mike slid Clara's hands from his shoulders, inviting her to wrap them tightly around his waist.

"No matter what we decide, it's me and you in it for the long hall. We're going to build a beautiful life together, Clara Covington. Just wait and see."

By late afternoon, Agnes had organized all things wedding related in the basement. The favors were arranged just so, the candle centerpieces were in boxes, ready to be unpacked. She had her checklist of duties as a maid of honor under control, ready to do anything she could to please her sister and make her happy.

"Agnes, everything looks amazing. I can't believe we're really pulling this off with such short notice," Clara said.

"I can. When you put your mind to something, you really

go after it. You actually made my job as maid of honor rather easy. The only thing I'm disappointed about is you choosing not to have a traditional shower. People want to celebrate you and Mike by showering you with gifts," she replied.

"I know, and they will shower us at the ceremony. You know me, Ag. I've always been rather simple and low-key. I'm actually surprised I didn't think of this whole thing a lot sooner than I did," Clara said, gazing over the favors.

"Well, if you're happy, I'm happy."

Holly, Clara's dog, sniffed around the boxes, wagging her tail when she approached Agnes.

"Apparently, Holly is happy too, so there you have it," she said, bending down to pet her.

"You might as well get used to hanging out with me, Holly. Your momma is going away for a little while."

Clara smiled. "I'll be sure to write down her feeding regiment. Thanks so much for looking after Holly, the house, and the warehouse. It really means a lot. Mike was a little nervous about being gone for two weeks, but I reassured him everything will be fine."

"It will be. I want you two to kick up your feet in Maui and relax. Just enjoy being husband and wife without the demands of running a business. Trust me, it will all be waiting for you when you get back."

"True." Clara comfortably pulled up a chair while helping Agnes unpack a box of candles.

"So, I haven't heard you say much about Grant lately. How are things going with you guys?"

"It's been fun getting to know him. He recently finished his last novel, and luckily, before he could pack his bags, his publisher asked him for the first two chapters of his next book. Having the two additional weeks was a pleasant surprise." Just talking about him made her flush in the face. It was almost inevitable the longer they had time together, the more she would develop feelings for the guy. What's not to like about him? He was a gentleman, unlike the guys in her past. He had depth to him. She wanted to experience more of his depth, and more of his sense of humor, but she knew it would soon end.

"Why haven't we spent time with him yet? I feel you're keeping him hidden. All I hear about these days is the food truck and the warehouse. That's it," Clara said.

"If it will make you feel any better, he's coming over in a little while. Well, technically, he's meeting me at the warehouse. He's been dying to see the truck, and since it's conveniently parked out back, I promised him I'd give him a little tour."

"Again, why haven't I met him yet?" Clara nudged.

"Let's be realistic here. It's not like he's going to be around forever, Clara. It's my luck that I would meet a truly phenomenal man who's just passing through Solomons, on the way to his next adventure. I see no point in getting deeply entrenched, allowing my feelings to go all willy-nilly out of control, only for him to inevitably say goodbye. No. I will not do it to myself. We're just friends. Maybe even two people who are attracted to one another and get along very well. But, it's not our time. Not everything works out the way they do in a romance novel." She sighed.

Clara laughed and laughed, and laughed some more, before finally regaining her composure.

"Bravo," she said.

"What?"

"That was an award-winning speech. I love it. You sound like a woman who has it all figured out. Except, the only problem is, you don't." Clara's chuckle faded.

"I'm not saying anything that isn't true. He is leaving soon, which means there's no sense in introducing him to family and getting my hopes up. What's so far-fetched about that state-ment?" Agnes asked, folding her eyebrows like an accordion.

"The only problem is you two already have feelings for one another. Just about every other night you're together. You think I don't notice when you come in late?" She teased.

Agnes didn't respond, but quietly contemplated what Clara was saying. She was right. But Maryland wasn't home for Grant. He wanted to see the world. That's what brought him there in the first place, and ultimately it would cause him to leave.

"Agnes, wake up. Look at what's happening right before your very eyes. He was supposed to be gone already. Now, his time is extended by another two weeks. Do you really think that's a coincidence?" she asked.

"His publisher really slammed the next project on him with little notice."

"Ag," she said, leaning in closer. "The details don't matter. The point is, he's still here. Make the most of it. I want to see him at the wedding, as your date. No questions asked."

"The wedding? Wouldn't you rather me just have him stop by for a casual burger on the grill?"

"That too. Even though we'll hardly have time for grilling this week. But you, my dear, need a date. So, invite him!"

Clara stood up, looking proudly over the work she'd done.

"Now, today is the reopening of the café, and if I know right, Mack has probably been spinning herself around like a lunatic. Maybe you can freshen up and join me over there before you go to meet your beau."

Agnes fluffed her hair playfully. "I don't mind if I do."

# CHAPTER 12

*M*ackenzie went through the motions of greeting customers, feeling relieved at the sight of Clara and Agnes walking in. She'd been waiting patiently to unleash details of the day's events, and she wasn't talking about the reopening. Everything at the café was going well, back in full swing, with everyone enjoying themselves as they did before the fire. It was her surprise visitor that was giving her anxiety.

"There you are. I was hoping you hadn't forgotten about me," she said, reaching out, hugging Clara first.

"I wouldn't dare. As promised, I gave you some time to prepare for the newspaper this morning, and time for you to get back into the swing of things." She looked around, admiring the turnout. "Looks like everyone missed being here, but we already knew Solomons would be here to support your big day," she said, beaming at the crowd.

Agnes nodded. "Honestly, would you look at this place? It's like the fire never happened. Hey, how's Beth making out next door? Do you think she'll be ready to open up soon?"

"She has a few more weeks before she's up and running.

Poor thing is going crazy with all the extra time on her hands. I can totally relate. I offered to lend a helping hand, but she says her contractors seem to have everything under control. For me, it's back to serving the regulars, including the bridge club who showed up on their off day, just to show their support. I'm feeling pretty lucky," Mack replied.

Clara stretched her arms open wide. "I'm so happy for you, Mack."

"Thank you, love. And I'm happy for you. Don't think for one minute, amid all this activity, that I'm going to miss that beachfront wedding of yours. Myself, Brody, and Steph will be there with bells on," Mackenzie replied.

"I know you will. Speaking of Brody, I swear I never see the guy these days. That's pathetic, given that we work for the same company. I promise, when Mike and I get back from Hawaii, we're releasing him back to his regular duties so he can catch a breather. This way you two can get back to your regular lives." Clara promised.

"Oh, it's fine. The three of us still spend time together. Besides, Brody is really good about adjusting when he has to. However —" Mackenzie checked over her shoulder, then lowered her voice.

"I'm not sure how he'll adjust after he finds out about the visit I had from Stephanie's father this morning." Mack confessed.

Agnes had a curious expression smeared across her face. "I haven't been around that long, but I don't recall you mentioning anything about Stephanie's father. I thought maybe the guy was... you know."

"Dead? Not a chance. He's alive and well and was standing right here in the doorway of the café this morning, right in front of Stephanie and Brody," Mack said.

A customer interrupted them, congratulating Mackenzie

on her grand reopening and promised to return soon. "The food was delicious, hun. Next time, I'll have to bring my mother. She needs to get out of the house more often."

"Oh, I can't wait to meet her. Thank you for coming. We'll see you soon." Mackenzie waved.

Once the lady left, she observed Dakota taking care of a couple sitting in the back and Joshua doing his usual rounds. Feeling at ease, she continued to talk to the girls.

"So, like I was saying. He's alive and well and was standing right in this very spot this morning. It was all I could do to keep it together. I felt like I was either going to pass out or lose my breakfast all over the floor. Neither option being a great start to the day. Thankfully, Brody was on his way out the door to take Stephanie to school for me." She explained.

"Wait. Brody has no idea who he is?" Clara asked.

"He was suspicious. But I played it off and got them out the door. I told him I'd explain later."

Agnes' eyes popped wide open. "This is surreal. I thought my life had its twists and turns, but yours is way more interesting. I ought to tell Grant to write about stuff like this in his book."

"Agnes, that's terrible," Clara said, fussing at her.

"No, she's right. I'm still in shock. He said he looked me up about six months ago, but never worked up the nerve to call. He's supposedly in Maryland for two nights, and I guess one of the first stops on his list this morning was the café. Of all places."

Mack swallowed and continued to put on her best possible smile as customers passed her by. On the inside, she was crying. She wanted to be by herself, hiding in a closet until this whole day that felt like a never-ending nightmare ended.

"Are you okay? Of all the days..." Clara said.

"No. I'm not okay, but I have no choice but to try my best

and push it out of my mind for now. I wouldn't listen to a word he had to say. I explained that this was a huge day for my business, and that he was five years behind schedule. That's when he turned around and walked right out the door. The same way he'd come in. There's no telling if he'll come back later or not. All I know is the whole thing has me worried sick. What if he wants to meet Steph? It's bad enough he had a chance to see her when she was leaving with Brody."

"Take a deep breath and then exhale," Clara said.

Agnes nodded in agreement. "Listen to her. She's amazing when it comes to yoga and breathing techniques. My mind wanders, but Clara is like the queen of all things whoosah related."

Mack and Clara looked at Agnes.

"Whoosah?" Mack asked.

"Yes, as in calming your nerves, relaxing, taking a chill pill. You know what I mean. Hey, all I'm saying is listen to her. She knows what she's doing."

Mack followed Clara's lead, taking a deep breath in, then exhaling before having to excuse herself to attend to a customer who was ready to check out.

Within the hour, Agnes drove her car down the dirt road leading to the warehouse. She pulled up behind the rear of a station wagon and could see Grant's smile in his rear-view mirror, greeting her as she arrived.

*Hmm, a station wagon. I guess he has a practical side to him, after all*, she thought to herself while putting the gear in park.

This time his appearance was even more casual than usual, making jeans and a button-down gingham shirt look like the most scrumptious outfit she'd ever seen him wear before.

"Hey," he said, approaching to open her car door.

"Hi."

She noticed a light beard growing in, replacing his clean-shaven look, and his dimples that were irresistibly cute. But it was the fresh scent of soap emanating from his body that gave her goosebumps.

Grant kissed her on the cheek. "I was hoping I had the right place. A guy stopped me on his way out, wondering why I was hanging around, until I introduced myself," he said.

"Oh, that was probably either Brody or the new guy, Ben."

He pointed upward. "Yeah, Ben. That's his name. I told him I was waiting for you."

She smiled, uncertain why she was smiling, but she knew it felt right.

"Is that your food truck over there?"

"It is. Would you like to see it?"

"Lead the way. I have to check it out first before giving you the gift that I brought. I have to make sure it's a just right fit," he said.

"Gift? You didn't have to bring me anything."

"I wanted to. And, from what I can see from here, I think it will be perfect. She's a beauty."

"Do you like her? I tried to go with something that would fit the whole barbecue theme, yet give off an old-fashioned food truck vibe at the same time." She smiled.

"Mission accomplished. The best part about it is I bet bbq will be in high demand out here. It doesn't look as if you have a lot of competition."

"Thankfully, I don't. I've been testing out various recipes, making specialty sauces and really trying to hone in on being creative and making it my own. I want people to taste my food and talk about it for days, telling all their friends, and coming back for more."

She opened the back door, welcoming him to look around.

"When do you have time to test recipes if you're always working at the warehouse and planning?"

"Thankfully, I'm not always working at the warehouse. I have a flexible schedule, which allows me to do a bit of both. Look at you, Mr. Observant." She teased.

"I only pay close attention to things that interest me most," he said, sweeping his fingers across her chin.

"Wow, the truck is amazing. You have the whole setup from top to bottom. Are you doing this alone, or are you going to have some help?" he asked.

"Alone for now. The doors will open part-time in June, and I'll have to take it from there. If it goes well, then maybe I can keep up the pace year-round.

"For sure. I've seen plenty of food truck operations in the winter," he replied.

Agnes watched as Grant ran his fingers across the counter, appearing to believe in her dream just as much as she did. He then refocused on her, holding her hands in his. "Stay right here. I'll be right back," he said.

"Grant, wait."

"Hang on, I'll be back before you can blink."

She followed him with her eyes, watching out of the double window as he hurried to the car and lifted his trunk. He pulled out what appeared to be a sign and brought it back inside.

"For you," he said, out of breath, presenting the gift.

She ran her fingers across the metal custom sign that said 'open for business' on one side and 'closed' on the other.

"Grant, it's beautiful. How thoughtful of you," she said.

"It's just a little something to show my support. I love that you're going after what you want in life."

She tugged on his shirt. "So are you. If anything, I'm encouraged and inspired by your journey. Unlike myself, you didn't stumble your way to this point, allowing challenges to distract you. It took me a long time to get to the place where I could even stay focused long enough to start working on my dreams."

He snickered. "Please don't think that I arrived here overnight. I fumbled, almost giving up quite a few times."

He took the sign out of her hands and placed it on the counter, inviting her to snuggle closely against him. "Tell me something," he said.

"What do you want to know?"

He thought long and hard.

"Walk me through the experiences you've had... the challenges that you always speak of in such a mysterious way."

Agnes felt an air of sadness wash over her. She wasn't proud of her journey. It wasn't as squeaky clean as his, but she figured, what did she have to lose?

She retreated from his arms and gazed over at the sign.

"Well, let's see. For starters, I moved here after a nasty breakup with my sister's ex-husband. How's that for a challenge?" she said, laughing with a nervous energy about her. "Bet you didn't see that coming. I know it doesn't sound good, and I'm certainly not proud of it. The only reason I have enough nerve to tell you in the first place is because I know you're leaving soon." Again, she chuckled, but he just continued to listen.

"Clara and I hadn't seen each other in several years. Almost ten, to be exact. We parted ways over what I would now consider to be absolute foolishness. Unresolved turmoil that began right around the time of our parents' death. What a time to stop getting along," she said.

Inside, her heart was racing, wondering what kind of judgement call he was making about her, but it was too late at this point.

"Anyway, long story short, I ran into Keith when we were both emotionally weak. Although I can now see how very wrong we were for each other, I still dated him. We were together all the way until the point at which he cheated on me, leaving me with nowhere to go. Pathetic, I know. But that's what led me here. Even prior to that, I had some track record. I really knew how to pick em." She confessed.

Grant's face was expressionless, making it difficult for her to read him. She'd understand if what she shared was off-putting. It was one of the reasons she'd decided not to be bothered with dating. She didn't want to spend the rest of her life being known as the woman with poor judgment. Not even to herself.

"Please, say something. It's difficult being this transparent, not knowing what you're thinking," she said.

"Is that the kind of man you desire to be with today? Someone who doesn't appreciate your heart, intelligence, your beauty, and your talent? Someone who'd be willing to take advantage of you by cheating with another woman?"

"Well, no. Of course not. What I wanted was a forever love. Someone to spend the rest of my life with. I just didn't go about it the right way. I guess I was too caught up in my insecurities to realize that I deserved better."

"Hmm. I'd have to agree that you deserve better. We both do. The question is, what are we willing to do about it? Are you going to spend the rest of your life feeling guilty over past mistakes? Am I going to spend the rest of my life sour over a woman who left me for someone else? Doesn't seem like the most productive way to spend our time, does it?" he asked.

"No."

He slid his hand by her side, drawing her closer to him. The mere touch of him brushing up against her sent chills up her arm.

Grant cupped her cheek with his other hand. "Good. I'm glad we can both agree. Now, what about this sabbatical of yours?"

"What about it? I thought maybe I needed some time to clear my head and focus on everything you see around you," she said, waving at the contents of the truck.

"I think it's an excuse for you to hide. It's only natural to retreat when you've been wounded. The only problem is, how are you going to ever experience genuine love by hiding behind old wounds?"

He stood within inches of her lips.

"I'm not hiding." She confided.

"Prove it. I've been pursuing you for months now, longing for an opportunity to get closer to you. Now, here we are. Please say you'll reconsider the sabbatical. I want us to be together."

Finally, the talking ceased, and their lips intertwined. At first gently, then passionately, before Agnes could regain her senses, figuring out the best way to respond.

"Grant. We can't be together. We were lucky to have this time, but you're leaving soon, and I don't know if I can withstand a quick rendezvous with an unhappy ending. I want more for myself. Especially after everything I've been through."

She regulated her breathing back to its normal cadence and tried to pull herself together.

"You are moving on to your next destination in the next two weeks, aren't you?"

"Yes, but —"

"And where would that destination be again? Nevada?" she asked.

"Yes, but it's only for a month this time. I can plan to come back and visit afterward."

"Grant, that's sweet and all, but I'm not looking for a visitor. Perhaps you were just curious about me, or maybe you enjoyed pursuing a woman who wasn't so easy to catch. I don't know. But look at where it's gotten us. We have feelings for each other and you're leaving. This is not going to work. We might as well save ourselves now and —"

Grant reached out to stop her. "Agnes, don't do it. Do not say something you know we'll both regret."

# CHAPTER 13

*J*onathan Middleton sat inside the cabin of their boat, gazing proudly at the wooden accents and recent upgrades. They'd sailed up to Annapolis after a hard day's work, putting in overtime at Lighthouse Tours. Parking at their friend's marina was a welcomed treat, allowing him alone time to relax and dream with Mae, and giving them a change in scenery.

"Jonathan, only you would think of a spontaneous trip at the last minute. As if you didn't spend the entire day on the water while giving your fishing tours," she said.

"I didn't have you by my side. I was with strangers all day, and while they were very nice, it doesn't compare to being with my wife."

He could feel her smiling at him as she passed along his dinner out of a cooler.

"Here's your ham sandwich, as requested. Not exactly a five-star gourmet meal, but it will do."

He reached for the sandwich plus a napkin. "Did you bring along my potato chips and my cookies?"

"Yes, dear. I knew I'd never hear the end of it if I didn't. It really got me to thinking about our trip next month with the kids. I'll need to make a list, ensuring they have everything they like to eat," Mae replied.

"I'm looking forward to our time with them."

"So am I. Even Lily is excited to see you in action. I didn't realize it until she said something, but she's never been sailing with you before."

"In that case, I'll see that she gets first class treatment. Only the best for your daughter and the grands... only the best." He chuckled.

They settled in, watching other people come and go. Some were strolling, others stopping to take in the early spring-like weather, while admiring the boats.

"It seems like not too long ago we rented my old pal Doc's yacht, and sailed the night away, making sweet memories under the stars," Jonathan said, winking at Mae.

He may have aged over the years, but the one thing that was still healthy and vibrant was his love and desire for his bride. He admired her beauty, her femininity, the meticulous way she kept her hair and maintained her manicure. He loved all that was good about her, plus her imperfections and flaws, and he didn't mind spoiling her occasionally to show it.

"We could've been ordering your favorite dish by now, if you would've allowed me to take you out, you know," he said.

"I know, honey. But there's something to be said about enjoying a quiet evening with you, just listening to the soothing sound of the water. Maybe even taking a stroll down the board-walk later on. I'm not in the mood for the hustle and bustle of a busy restaurant tonight. Besides, packing the cooler was easy. You know I love taking care of you."

"Woman, if I wasn't eating this sandwich, I'd come right over there and —"

"Now, now, tiger. They'll be plenty of time for that." She teased.

They sat a while longer, finishing up their food and making plans for how they would spend the rest of the evening. However, there was something lingering in the back of Jonathan's mind, nudging him for days that he needed to get off his chest.

"Mae."

She looked up while still finishing the rest of her beverage.

"There's something I need to tell you. Something that's been bugging me for a little while," he said.

"Okay."

"Do you remember the afternoon we were sitting in the garage, talking about Edith?" he asked.

"Yes." He noticed Mae's facial expression quickly changing to a look of concern.

"There's no need to worry. I just thought you would want to know everything she shared with me the day I was over there, fixing her sink."

"I'm listening," Mae said.

He took a deep breath. "I asked what brought her to Solomons Island. You know, making small talk on the way down to the hardware store. It's typically what you do when you don't know someone."

"Mm hmm."

"She told me she was divorced and starting over again, after her husband left her. And it got me to thinking —"

"What did it get you to thinking, Jonathan?" She snarled.

"Mae, be nice, please." He chuckled. "Absolutely nothing happened. We were just exchanging small talk, as I said earlier. But a woman like that... well, she's probably very lonely, and I'll bet she could really use a friend, Mae. I know you invited her to get to know Meredith, but I honestly can't think of a better person than yourself to invite her out and show her around the island."

Mae grunted.

"Around the island? If she wants a tour, we offer those six days a week at the job. I'm sure we can even get her a discount, Jonathan."

"Mae Middleton, that's not what I mean, and you know it. Think about how life was for you when you first lost your husband," he said.

"That was different. The man died, he didn't leave me. Two completely different scenarios."

"Yes, with one very important thing in common. You felt all alone back then, and if my discernment is leading me correctly, she's feeling alone now."

He watched as Mae fiddled around with the items she packed in the cooler, not really doing much, except for keeping herself busy.

"I'm surprised at you, Mae. You normally have such a big heart toward helping others," he said.

"And that hasn't changed. I'm helping Clara with her decorations for the ceremony later on this week, and I offered a seat at our table during the holidays for Meredith. You know me well enough to know that I'll help anyone in need. But Edith is different. Maybe it's because I don't know her well enough yet, but us women usually have a sixth sense about these things."

In response, Jonathan laughed uncontrollably, probably one of the worst things he could've done. But he did, making Mae even more annoyed.

"I'm sorry, Mae. Come on. Come over here and sit next to me," he said, tugging at her hand.

"I'm glad you find so much humor in all this, but I'm serious, Jonathan. It doesn't hurt to take your time getting to know certain people. That way, you can figure out if they're trust-worthy or not."

He continued to smile, shaking his head, agreeing whole-heartedly.

"This is true. And I never want to undermine your feelings. All I was trying to suggest is maybe you could get to know her... on your terms, of course. Also, just so you know, there's nothing behind my request other than me detecting she could probably use a good friend. Out of the two of us, you're a more appro-priate fit."

Mae nestled next to him, sliding her hand across his back. "I know. You're just being the kind soul I fell in love with. You've always had a big heart, Jonathan. If it means that much, I'll see if she wants to come along the next time I go shopping in town. Or maybe she'd enjoy a visit to the café. Nothing forced. Just a casual invite will do."

Jonathan responded with a subtle smile. "Thank you, dear."

"Brody, what would I do without you? Thank you so much for taking Steph home for me. All you have to do is remind her to get a head start on her homework and tell her I'm going to double- check it. I should be home no later than nine-thirty," Mack said, talking into the speaker phone of her cell in one hand while holding a broom in the other.

Day one of her re-opening had been just as successful as she'd hoped it would be. With the anticipation behind her and everyone gone for the evening, she could now focus on cleaning up for the evening and closing as she normally would.

*I literally just went from boredom to pure exhaustion in a matter of a day.*

*Well, you'd prayed for a thriving business, so don't complain.*

Joshua pushed through the double doors and removed his hat, looking just as exhausted as she felt.

"Another day at Mack's Café in the books. Turned out to be a spectacular grand opening, if you ask me. Couple that in conjunction with the feature in the newspaper, I can only imagine what the extra exposure is going to do for business," he said.

Mackenzie held the broom in place, contemplating the new name.

"Mack's Café. Hmm. That has an interesting ring to it. I might have to keep it in mind should I ever decide to change the name in the future," she said.

"I would. It's sounds personal. People will feel connected because they all know Mack."

"You know something, Joshua. You're great as a server, but you really do have a knack for business as well. I hope you're still working hard at pursuing your goals with your online auto business."

He perked up, standing proud. "Thanks. I'm still chipping away at it. I find for now it's much easier to list the parts on websites that allow you to sell across the country. That way, the only overhead I ever need to be concerned about is the fees. Maybe one day I can grow it to the point of opening up a brick and mortar. But, don't worry, if that day comes, I'd give you plenty of warning time."

"I know you would." She smiled.

The front door opened, drawing their attention to the man who had entered the café at the start of the day. Mackenzie could feel herself gripping the broom even tighter but tried not to show any change in expression on her face.

"Good evening, Mackenzie," the man said, removing his hat.

"Alexander," she replied, noticing in her peripheral that Joshua was planted comfortably by the register.

"I thought I'd stop back by, given that this morning you had a lot going on. Do you think we could talk?" the man asked.

"I can't imagine after all these years we'd have anything to talk about. Besides, I have to clean up and get out of here soon."

"Mackenzie, I beg to differ. We have a daughter together. There's plenty to discuss."

She noticed Joshua's mouth drop open. He looked as if he was silently screaming, if there was such a thing.

"Joshua, it's okay for you to head home. I'll take over from here," she said.

"You sure? I can help clean up in the back if you want me to."

"No. It's fine. Head home and get some rest. It's going to be a long day tomorrow." Mack's eyes lowered, fighting the burning sensation in her eyes.

Once Joshua left, Alex seated himself at a booth, awkwardly waiting for her to join him.

"I'm fine standing here," she said.

"I know you're probably upset with me, Mackenzie, and you have every right to be. Showing up in your lives after a six-year absence is a huge deal."

"Hmm."

"I realize how selfish I was to leave, pursuing my career over family. There's no excuse that will make up for what I've done. But there's also no excuse for me to continue to stay away, not trying to right my wrongs." He looked at her with the same puppy dog eyes he'd given her when he begged for her support in starting his band. She fell for it back then. But she wasn't falling for it now.

Mackenzie let out a sigh mixed with exhaustion and a bit of 'I couldn't care less' in it.

"Is that all?"

"Yes, but there's a lot to unpack in what I just stated, Mack," he replied.

"It's Mackenzie to you. I see some things haven't changed, the main thing being self-centeredness. You didn't really expect that you could come by my place of business twice, and I would just drop everything and cater to your wishes, did you?"

"I didn't know what to expect. But I knew I had to come. Look, hear me out. Although I went about it the wrong way, my life is better off now. The guys and I travel across the country getting steady gigs and making a real comfortable income. I mean, real comfortable. I can contribute financially, making things easier on you. And, in exchange, I just ask that I get to know her. I want our girl to know that I'm her dad," he said.

Mackenzie put the broom down, feeling somewhat over-heated. "How can she get to know someone who travels all the time, never settled down in one place long enough to create a meaningful relationship? The only time you come up in conversation is when she's being teased by her friends in school, Alex. Do you know what they're teasing her about?"

"No."

"She's the only one among her friends who doesn't have a dad involved in her life," she responded.

He hung his head low. "I see."

"Mm hmm."

"I figured the conversation would go like this, but I'm still not backing down, Mackenzie. I won't pressure you to move at my pace. Only you know what Stephanie can handle and at what pace. But, when the time is right, I want to meet her. I want her to know she has a father who cares. A real father, unlike the guy who carried her out of here this morning."

Feelings of infuriation on Mack's part were an understatement. *Who was he to waltz into their lives after practically being gone since birth?* And how dare he make a comment about Brody? A man who'd been present since the day he met Stephanie.

"I'd like to think I've made some good decisions regarding Stephanie and who she spends time with. The man you're referring to, he's one of those good decisions. Steph looks up to him as a father figure. So, be real careful about where you cast stones."

He lifted his hands apologetically.

"Okay, fair enough. I overstepped my boundaries. It won't happen again."

His voice faded as she recalled images of the day he left. Back then, it was just supposed to be a week away with the band. A well thought out trip, that she agreed to. An opportunity that would help jump start their fame, giving them a name in a much larger city. Of course, they'd travel sometimes, doing weekend shows, but he'd return home, as promised, spending more time at home than away. At least, that's what she was told. He would be his own boss, able to dictate his schedule, and that was one of the selling points that allowed her to be supportive. Sadly, that's not the way things went.

"Mackenzie, are you all right?"

She stuttered. "No, I'm not all right. I really don't think you considered what kind of impact this reemergence into our lives would have. I'm still dumbfounded that you could walk in here today, really expecting that I would go along with anything that you have to say. How do I know this isn't some sort of a whimsical idea that will soon fade the moment you get back on the road? Two days isn't hardly enough time for a little girl to understand. Plus, I don't know who you are anymore, Alex. I don't know where you've been, or who you're spending time with. No way, this is crazy."

"Mackenzie."

"No. I would never entertain a stranger spending time with my daughter, so how are you any different?" she asked.

He drew his hat to his chest, speaking words that touched the very core of her soul.

"I'm her father. As lame as it may sound, it's still the truth. And for the record, I know in your eyes I'm a complete jerk. I get it. But I would never request that I meet Stephanie in two days and then leave. She's going to have so many questions, and that would be downright cruel. I have a signed contract requiring me to be here one week per month, playing at National Harbor."

"A casino job?"

"Yes, I guess you could call it that. Although they're also known for their concerts and entertainment. Anyway, I'd like to talk with you and get reacquainted, hoping eventually you would allow me to reconnect with Steph. I'm leaving my card here on the table with my number. As always, it's your call. Although as I mentioned, I have no intentions of easily giving up."

She watched him place the card on the table before making eye contact one last time.

"Mackenzie, please think about it. I was completely wrong for what I did, acting like a child without responsibilities. But I've changed, and I'm prepared to be a man, owning up to the error of my ways. I'm leaving tomorrow, but I'll be back. I'll gladly take your call on the road or when I'm in town," he said, then slipped out the door just as quietly as he'd slipped in.

# CHAPTER 14

*A*gnes Covington stirred frantically, trying to recapture the right mix of ingredients. She woke up with a brilliant idea to advertise her signature sauce options on a sign outside the truck. She'd offer the public a variety, ranging from mild and sweet, to Texas hot and spicy, one of her specialties. If only she could repeat a recipe she created earlier in the week. If only she could concentrate, not thinking about her last conversation with Grant, then she might make some progress.

*Come on, Agnes. Something is missing*, she said to herself, sounding annoyed.

"I'll tell you what's missing. It's your sanity, that's what's missing! It's four o'clock in the morning, just three hours before the make-up artist arrives for the wedding. What on earth are you doing? And why does the kitchen look like a war zone?" Clara asked.

"I'm sorry. I was tossing and turning and decided to come down and try out a few recipe ideas. I didn't wake you, did I?"

Clara dipped her finger in the cup with the darkest sauce, helping herself to a sample.

"Mmm, that one is a keeper. Pass me the cup over there," she said, smacking her lips. "You didn't wake me. I also couldn't sleep. I'm so nervous about properly reciting my vows that I'm having a hard time allowing my mind to rest."

"Well, that's an easy fix. Why don't you just write your vows on a small piece of paper and read it aloud? Duh!"

"Noo... I will not write them down. I want to look into Mike's eyes and hold his hands, making it as special as possible. It's important to me."

"Okay, but I don't think Mike would want you to lose sleep over it. I'm just saying." Agnes laughed.

She stared in the pantry, looking for something that might give her a little inspiration.

"I'm proud of you, Ag. I've literally watched you grow so much since you arrived here. I know your food truck is going to be a success. I honestly don't see why you don't open up for business next week."

"Why, thank you. That means a lot coming from you, sis. But, for one, I refuse to open up until I too, have mastered this thing to perfection. Plus, you and Mike need all hands on deck between Lighthouse Tours and the warehouse. So, I think I'll stick to my starting date of June first." She smiled.

"True. We do need all hands on deck. By the way, Mike has been raving about you. He says you're a natural and wishes he could promote you to run the place. Don't worry, I strongly discouraged it, reminding him you need your free time to run a business of your own."

"Thank you. I'm glad he's happy, but yes, I appreciate the free time. I'm going to need every minute of it in just a short while," she said.

Clara nudged Agnes on the arm. "Hey, you haven't mentioned a word about your date. He is coming, isn't he?"

Agnes picked up the pace, closing the door to the pantry

and wiping down the counters. The less she had to talk about it, hopefully, meant the more she could push through, moving on with her life as it was prior to meeting Grant.

"No."

"Agnessss. I recognize that look. What happened?"

"Nothing, everything is fine. I'm just staying focused on your special day, that's all. Besides, you'll probably need me, which means I would have very little time to spend with a date, anyway."

Clara rolled her eyes. "Hold on. I'm not buying that answer for a second. I'm having a very small wedding on the beach in our backyard. What is there to do besides stand beside me and look pretty for the photos? Okay, maybe fix my train if it gets disheveled and pass me the ring, but that's about it. After that, we're all heading back to the tent to party. So, what's your hang up again?"

Agnes' mind flashed back to the moment where she reversed away from Grant's car, watching him standing there after saying her goodbyes.

"Agnes? Hello, earth to mars. What's the issue?"

"Grant won't be able to make it. He's leaving today for his next destination." She fibbed, hoping this would shift the attention on to more important things, like the wedding.

"Aww, Ag. I'm so sorry. Did he say he would stay in touch? I'm sure you guys could video chat until you see each other again," Clara said.

"I don't think that will work. I've never been good at in-person relationships, let alone a long distance one. It's not really my cup of tea."

"I hear ya, kiddo, but I think you're being a little hard on yourself. I don't believe in never, and I don't think you should put much stock in it yourself. I never thought I would get married. I grew very comfortable being a housekeeper to a woman who became my best friend. But, here I am, getting married to a man who I met by backing into his car. A man who graciously offered me a job when I was out of work and needed it most. Do you know how often Joan and I used to talk about me meeting the right one and falling in love? Ha, I used to laugh at her, saying, okay, Joan, that's sweet and all, but let's get back to reality here."

"Why did you doubt what she was saying?" Agnes asked.

"Because, after I left New York, I grew accustomed to keeping up my walls of protection from ever being hurt again, somewhat like yourself. I figured if I focused on my job, then that was enough. I didn't have time for men."

Agnes continued wiping the counters, slowing down at the last few words that Clara spoke.

"You mean you were protecting yourself from ever being hurt by Keith again? He's the reason you didn't want to get involved with anyone else."

Clara nodded. "Yep. Now that you put it that way, he was a major part of the problem. There's something about that man that has a way of leaving a woman feeling so —"

"Bitter at the idea that you were ever gullible enough to be with him in the first place?" she asked.

"Right. That's part of it, but also, he just made me want to be independent. Free from all the crap he was dishing out. He made me want to prove to myself that I could get out there and make it on my own. And so I did. But, almost to a default. You don't want that for yourself, Agnes. Trust me, it's a lonely path you're heading down if you're not careful. I loved my boss like she was my family. She truly became like a best friend, taking me in when I needed it most. But that kind of friendship could never replace the love that comes from your forever person, and Joan knew it. That's why she used to encourage me to get out there and meet people. I was just too stubborn to listen. I wasted ten years not listening to her advice. Ten long, stubborn years."

Agnes cracked a smile. "Hey, we're Covington women. That means we're headstrong, sometimes, but everything always works out in the end, right? At one o'clock this afternoon, you're about to prove that things do work out in the end."

Clara ruffled up her sister's hair and then held her by the cheeks. "Do you know how many women would die for an opportunity to be with someone like Grant?"

"I'm sure the number would be pretty high."

"Mm hmm. And even that is an understatement. Do me a favor. Don't wait ten years like I did being stubborn and having to live with many regrets. Go after him and apologize for kicking him to the curb."

Agnes widened her eyes. "Who said anything about —"

"Shh. You're my flesh and blood. I know better. You kicked him to the curb and now you have to fix it. So, call him up, catch a flight. I don't care what you have to do. The one thing I know for certain is the guy already has your heart. You're falling for him, and I see absolutely no reason to let a good man like that get away."

"Clara, I'm not going anywhere today, except to your wedding. If it's meant to be then we'll speak again." Agnes frowned.

"Ooh, you're so stubborn, just like our father."

"And you're so hardheaded, just like our father," Agnes said, sticking out her tongue.

The two laughed hysterically, collapsing in each other's arm for a big hug.

"Speaking of our parents, I have a wedding gift for you. It's something I think mom would've wanted you to have," Agnes said.

She went to the living room and returned with a stack of blue boxes joined with white ribbon.

"You didn't have to get me anything, Agnes. Having you there with me was all I ever needed."

"Nonsense. You need something borrowed and something blue. Now, I realize you guys want to have a special ceremony here at the house, tossing tradition to the wind. But, some things cannot be overlooked, and this is one of them. Open your gift."

She watched as Clara removed the gift wrap, one by one, unpacking special items she'd saved after their parents passed away.

"Mom's pearl earrings and her blue satin handkerchief. I completely forgot about these," Clara said, tearing up a bit.

"Well, I didn't. If mom were here today, I know she would want you to have them."

Agnes held her sister close, feeling thankful for their rekindled relationship, and thankful to be a part of her wedding. The exchange between sisters that once could've been deemed as unforgivable was buried and had been for a while now. In its place was a bond, one that couldn't be broken again, and one that would forever carry on the memory of their beloved mother and father.

A member of the waitstaff rolled around a delectable dessert cart, serving wedding cake to the guests. All the women wore spring colors, some with floral accents that blended beautifully with their partners. It was a picture-perfect day. One that Agnes realized she hoped to experience at her own wedding someday. It was a new thought, but one she could get used to.

"Ms. Mae, you look absolutely stunning. You and Jonathan make such a lovely couple," Agnes said.

"Why, thank you, Agnes. Where's your beau? Everybody at Lighthouse Tours has been dying to meet him."

A ridiculous feeling of embarrassment washed over her, showing up in her red cheeks.

"Who are you speaking about?"

Ms. Mae leaned in.

"Agnes, everybody knows that you and the author have a thing for one another. The only one trying to keep it a secret is you."

Agnes turned around, checking to see that no one else was listening. She didn't know why. It was rather silly, and perhaps a remanent of her previous indecisive behavior.

"He's not coming today. We had a little tiff. Turns out we're not on the same page about long distant relationships, with one of us being against it more than the other." She confessed.

Had Agnes ever really been in a long distant relationship before? No. But, she wanted to avoid any possibilities of cheating or suffering from a lonely heart at all costs. If you can't actually be together, then what's the point of calling it a relationship? At least, that's what she believed.

"Interesting," Ms. Mae replied.

Jonathan interrupted their conversation, greeting Agnes. "Something tells me this is the perfect time for my wife and I to head to the dance floor. Spend one more minute on the topic and she'll have you deeply engaged in a therapeutic session about relationships." Jonathan teased.

Agnes laughed, watching him lead her away. "Don't worry, Ms. Mae, we'll have our time to talk," she said.

A member of the wait staff approached her. "Excuse me, are you Miss Agnes Covington?" she asked.

"Yes."

"There's a guest waiting for you out front. He said he didn't want to interrupt the party, but he was wondering if he could have a moment to speak with you."

She kept her smile to herself and checked for Clara and Mike first, ensuring they were happy. And, indeed, they were. Clara was glowing at the altar and on the dance floor, in love, and probably relieved to have the planning portion of her wedding behind her.

"Sure. I'll head up there now," she said.

Agnes maintained a steady pace in her high heels, trying her hardest not to wobble, as she allowed her nerves to get the best of her. If it was Grant, she'd apologize for the way their last conversation ended. Maybe they could figure something out, but for now, she just needed to see him.

"I was hoping it would be you," she said, pulling open the front door.

Ben, the new employee who was working with her at the warehouse, was waiting patiently on the other side. She noticed he cleaned up well in his suit and tie but wondered why he was at the front door instead of inside with the guests.

"Hey, Agnes, sorry to bother you. Mike made arrangements for me to allow one of his customers to pick up their boat," he said, jiggling keys in the air. "Everything is all set, but for some reason, the alarm is malfunctioning, and I can't get it to reset. I didn't want to bother the boss on his big day, but I was wondering if you could help me," he said.

The more he spoke, all her mind could calculate was Grant wasn't standing at the door. It drew her eyes to the ground and her heart felt like it was sagging.

"Agnes?"

"Uh, yeah. Sorry, I've been meaning to call a technician to come out and fix it. All you have to do is ignore the error and set the away code. Everything should work just fine after that," she responded.

"Perfect. I should be back in ten to fifteen minutes, tops."

"No problem. Take your time."

She thanked him and closed the door, feeling less than thrilled about returning to the party alone. Curling up under a blanket with a pint of ice cream would've been her preference, but it was her sister's wedding, so she returned, determined to get over herself.

"Agnes, there you are. Brody and I have been searching for you high and low so we could congratulate you on a job well done. Everything looks absolutely beautiful," Mackenzie said, giving her a squeeze.

"Ha, the compliment really belongs to Clara. You know how Clara is, she knows exactly how she like things. I can only take a little bit of the credit for the favors. You, on the other hand, sent over the most fabulous cake. I heard we owe Chef Harold a huge thank you," she replied.

"Yes, lucky for us, he's also a talented baker. When he heard Clara was doing something more intimate for the wedding, he gladly volunteered to send over a few cake samples."

Brody waved, standing beside Stephanie, who looked at him with complete adoration. In Agnes' eyes, they were a perfect fit, someday making an adorable little family.

"You know, this really is a quaint little island. Everyone is so tightly knit together, and I love the way everyone looks out for one another. It's very nice," Agnes replied.

"Oh, there's no place like it." Mack nodded.

After the reception, Agnes said her goodbyes to Mike and Clara, wishing them a safe flight in the morning. Then, she walked barefoot to the freezer, grabbing the pint of ice cream she'd been dreaming of and a spoon. After one scoop, her eyelids closed. Another scoop and her sorrows began melting away. It was a temporary thrill, but one that might at least help get her through the night, along with sweet Holly at her feet and a comfortable blanket.

"Let's go, girl," she said, beckoning for Holly to follow her to the basement. Downstairs, she checked her cell phone, but there were no missed calls, no text messages, and frankly, she didn't expect there to be. If she was in Grant's position, after all the effort he'd made to win her over, she probably wouldn't call either.

# CHAPTER 15

Mackenzie pulled the covers over Stephanie's shoulder, tucking her in, and turning out the lamp. She'd grown so much, yet at almost seven years old, she was still her little girl. The same girl who figured out how to climb out of the crib on her own, and when she was old enough, figured out how to climb to the top of the fridge to reach the chocolate chip cookies. In recent years, Mackenzie had just gotten used to the idea of sharing her daughter's affection with Brody. He had proven himself, and she knew he could be trusted. But her father? That was another story. How in the world would she explain to Steph or to Brody that her father was ready to be back in their lives?

*Goodnight, sweet girl,* she whispered, giving her a kiss. She closed the door, returning to Brody, who was waiting on the couch.

"Did she fall asleep?" he asked.

"Did she? She was knocked out the moment I stepped into her room. I can't blame her. She had a full day with the wedding and all. She was so excited to get dressed up and get out on the dance floor with her Aunt Clara and Uncle Mike. It made me realize, the kid doesn't get enough opportunities to dress up. I need to do something about that." She laughed.

"We'll have to be intentional in planning something special every now and again."

"Yeah." She sighed, resting her head on the couch and gazing up at the ceiling.

Brody began massaging her feet. "What about yourself? How are you holding up this weekend?"

"Me? I'm fine, couldn't be better. The reopening of the cafe was more than I could ask for, and Clara's wedding was absolutely lovely. I like the idea of having a small ceremony. I notice it's becoming more and more trendy, helping couples save money, and easing some of the stress."

Brody laughed. "Hey, if it's a small wedding you want, then a small wedding you shall have. But that's not what I'm referring to. How are you doing personally? You didn't seem like yourself earlier today. The only time you perked up was when we ran into someone or when spoken to, but that's not like you."

"Oh, I was probably just tired, that's all."

She adjusted herself on the couch, hoping her excuse would be sufficient.

"Mack, come on. Is there something you're not telling me? You haven't been yourself since the morning that guy showed up at the café."

"Brody, I'm fine." She snapped, immediately feeling guilty for taking on such a tone.

"Okay, I won't press it. I just wanted you to know that you could talk to me if something was bothering you," he said.

Immediately, tears fell. *Who am I kidding?* she thought to herself. One way or another Brody would have to know the truth, especially since they were growing closer, and perhaps even making plans for marriage someday.

"I'm sorry. I didn't mean to be short with you. I'm so frustrated I can't even think straight." She admitted, sitting upright, releasing a floodgate of tears.

Brody held her for several minutes, not saying a word, but simply comforting her instead.

"The man you saw this morning was Stephanie's father, Alex."

"What?"

"He showed up without warning. I was so nervous that Stephanie would become curious about him, so I said nothing, hoping she'd follow you out the door as soon as possible."

"Whoa, I didn't see that coming." He reached out, touching her hand.

"Mmm, that makes two of us. I'm still trying to wrap my mind around it. After all these years, there he is, standing at the door, wanting to know if I had time to talk with him. It felt like a bad dream, except it wasn't."

"Did he say what he wanted?"

"I sent him away the first time." She hesitated, knowing it might disappoint Brody that she kept this to herself.

"I told him we were having a big day and there was no time to talk, hoping that would be the end of it, but it was foolish of me to think such a thing. Why would a man travel miles, making it his business to find me, only to turn around and leave? It wouldn't make any sense."

As she spoke, she noticed Brody still holding her hand and being supportive. It was just what she needed.

"He returned at closing to sit down and talk with me."

"Wait a minute. At closing? Were you by yourself? I don't know that I like the idea of him showing up whenever he pleases."

She let out a faint chuckle. "Thank you, Brody, but I don't think you have to worry about my safety. He may be a deadbeat dad, but he wouldn't harm a fly. Plus, Joshua was there, but I ended up sending him home. It was way too much for me to handle with having someone else standing around listening."

Brody got out of his seat, appearing frustrated. "If I would've known who he was, I would've decked him one time for the way he abandoned you two, then another time for showing up unexpectedly and upsetting you."

"Brody, I'll be fine. It was just the initial shock of it all. Even though, now I can't stop thinking about his request to meet Stephanie. He said he has a gig playing at National Harbor once a month and he'd like to spend some time with her when he's in town. Brody, I can't just hand my baby over to him like that. I just can't."

Again, she flashed back to a time when Stephanie wasn't even knee high to a duck, still waddling around in diapers. Sure, those days were long over, but those were memories that only she could tuck away in the depths of her heart, not Alex. It almost seemed unfair to him to show up now. Yet, inevitably, Stephanie would develop an ever-growing curiosity about her dad someday.

"Baby, I'm so sorry you're going through this. The thought of it must eat you up inside. Now it makes sense why you were so distracted earlier. If you want me to talk to him, I'd be glad to. I'll send him a clear message that if he comes around and bothers you anymore, he'll have me to answer to," Brody said.

Mackenzie shook her head, trying to make sense of every-thing. She buried her face in her hands, letting out another good cry before pulling it together.

"I never thought the words would come out of my mouth. But I really have to sit down and think things through. I hate that this is happening. The whole thing makes me feel uneasy, but he is her father. If, for any reason, he wanted to escalate this to the court of law, then I might have trouble on my hands. I don't want it to get to that, Brody." She explained, wiping her face.

He ran his fingers through his hair, working just as hard as Mackenzie, trying to figure it out.

"Do you really think Stephanie will feel comfortable meeting him?"

She locked eyes with him. "I don't know. But, I'll tell you one thing, Stephanie never goes on a playdate without me first getting to know the parents. It's a rule I've always lived by, and I will not stop playing by the rules just because he woke up and decided he wants to be in her life again. There will be no introduction, not even a consideration of one, until I have more time to talk to him. It's the least he can do."

Immediately she detected a look of disappointment on Brody's face, which he tried to hide by heading into the kitchen.

"Brody, talk to me. It's not like you to walk away," she said.

"I don't know what to say. I feel kind of helpless, actually. I'm not Stephanie's guardian, and I'm not your husband. The only thing I can do is offer my support. Other than that, I don't have a leg in the race."

Her hands rested gently on his chest. "Don't say that. What you think matters to me. It's only a matter of time before we're a family, so you do have a leg in all this."

Mackenzie leaned in, offering a tender kiss. It was her way of reassuring him he played an important role in their lives. In her opinion, that wasn't about to change. The look of uncertainty disappeared from his face as he met her lips in return, teasing her at first, then kissing her passionately.

Mae flicked a match, lighting the last candle in their den. She had fifteen arranged around the room and one illuminating a bottle of wine. The sound of the shower stopped minutes ago, giving her an adrenaline rush, hoping everything would be perfect for her surprise to Jonathan.

"Jonathan, I'm in the den. Why don't you come down and join me?"

"I'll be there in a second," he yelled from a distance.

She felt pretty this evening, wearing a new silk pajama set, with her nails and toes freshly done. Choosing Jonathan's favorite shade of red always made him feel special and desired by her. Now, all she needed to do was create the right atmosphere for a romantic evening for two.

"Well, what do we have here?" Jonathan asked.

"Oh, just a few candles, a little wine, and me, of course." She wiggled her fingernails at him, instantly making him smile.

"Now, how am I supposed to stay focused with you looking so beautiful, Mae?"

"That's the point. You're not supposed to do anything but relax and enjoy a wonderful evening together."

She patted his favorite chair, inviting him to sit down.

"Mae, what's going on here? I'm normally the one who surprises you, not the other way around." He grumbled.

"Exactly. Don't you think it's about time I spoiled you for a change? Jonathan, you work hard giving tours for several hours a day —"

"So do you," he said.

"Let me finish. Yes, I work hard, but I don't have to deal with fishing rods, and coming home with an achy back due to all the bending and being around smelly men all day. You've sacrificed a lot, even working extra hours, so you spoil me the way you do. I just wanted to do something special for you in return. And, I also feel like I owe you an apology."

Jonathan signaled for her to join him. "Apologize for what, Mae?"

"My childish behavior. Heck, it's probably childishness mixed with envy. All I know is you were right the other day when you said I wasn't acting like myself. I haven't been and if I'm being honest, I think it's pure jealousy on my part. Edith is a gorgeous woman, and I can't stand that it bothers me so. But, it does." She confessed.

"Aw, Mae. As I told you before, I only have eyes for you."

"I know, Jonathan. You'd be proud to know that in order to combat my ridiculous feelings, I stopped by her place earlier today. I caught her working in the yard and offered to lend her a few of my garden tools. It wasn't much, but it's a start." She chuckled.

"That's the spirit."

She popped open the bottle of wine and poured a glass, passing it to him.

"You know, there was a time in my life where I would've been ashamed to admit that I was jealous of someone. If I was still in my twenties and thirties, I would've denied it to the end. Don't get me wrong, I think there's still something to be said about a woman's intuition. I still have my eye on Miss Edith, but that doesn't give me an excuse to change my character."

Mae passed him the glass and poured her own so they could toast. "This experience also taught me a valuable lesson regarding you, Jonathan."

"Me? Oh no, what did I do now?"

"You didn't do anything, dear. I'm just reminded how much I need to treasure you as my husband and shower you with all the attention that you deserve. If I were more focused on that instead of worrying about our neighbor, I doubt things would've ever gotten so out of hand."

Mae cracked up at the surprised look on Jonathan's face.

But she couldn't blame him. They'd known each other since their days of just being friends, and one thing she'd always been was stubborn, and not so quick to admit when she was wrong. Tonight, she wanted to put that behind her, creating a special evening that was all about Jonathan and nothing else. So, she proposed a toast to her husband and enjoyed a celebratory sip. Then she brushed her hand against his cheek, whispering softly, "I love you, Jonathan."

"I love you more. It means a lot that you would take the time to do this for me." He placed his glass down and held her by the waistline. "Let's forget about everything else and make this a special night to remember," he said, giving her soft pecks, sending heat to her neckline.

Mae adored their affection, which could be as innocent as a sweet kiss or as sensual as lovers together for the first time. She adored him and vowed to do everything she could to show it.

"Hello?" Agnes answered, holding the phone upside down. The slightest glimpse of daylight peered through the blinds. But then again, she was delusional, so she could've been imagining it was morning.

A man's voice spoke up. "Hi."

"Grant?"

"Yes, I'm sorry for calling so early."

It didn't take her long to wake up. She cleared her throat, immediately happy to hear his voice. How foolish she'd been not to dial his number before now, allowing pride to get in the way.

"No, you're fine. I was actually thinking about you."

"You were?" he asked.

"Yes."

He was quiet for a moment.

"Well, you probably wouldn't have caught me, anyway. I've been traveling the last couple of days and dealing with layovers and cancellations. I finally made it back home last night."

Disappointment washed over Agnes. She'd really done it this time, taking her foot and inserting it all the way into her mouth to the point of sending him back home.

"I'm sorry to hear that."

"Hey, it comes along with the territory. I made it to my publisher's office in time for an important meeting, so that had to count for something," he said.

Agnes sat up in bed, drawing the covers up to her chin.

"Look, I called because of the way we ended things. I have to be honest, it's been bothering me tremendously. I know you have your feelings about long distance relationships. If anyone has struggled with trusting and taking a leap of faith, it would be me, so I completely understand. But out of the two of us, I was still willing to be brave enough and try it. I packed my things and left, not because of a meeting, but because I couldn't stand the idea of being in Solomons and not being with you. I tried to write, but I couldn't focus. I went out for walks and grabbed coffee, but all I did was think of you. We had something special, Agnes, and I'm just sorry you allowed your fears to have the final say."

She was shocked. It seemed like another minute passed before she opened her mouth to breathe. "I don't know what to say. I was on a mission when I met you, Grant. I was focused. I never expected in a million years that I'd actually fall in —"

She froze. It was almost as if the voice in her head wanted to scream from the mountain tops that she'd fallen for him, but her vocal cords were struggling to let it out. Would she be revealing too much? she wondered. Would it even matter now that he'd packed his things and moved away?

"Why can't you say it?" he asked. "What's so terrible about admitting that although we weren't planning for it, we fell for each other?"

"Fine, I'll say it if you want me to. I fell for you, Grant. I've missed being with you, and I still wish that you were here. But, you know what, none of that matters because my life is here on Solomons Island, and your life is wherever your writing takes you. We live in two separate worlds, accidentally colliding over a cup of coffee that spilled all over your jacket. Love like that can't last," she said.

"That's not true."

Agnes hesitated, then boldly declared, "Well, then, one of us has to take a leap of faith."

Her mind drifted, wondering what a leap of faith would really look like in her world. Agnes hadn't envisioned herself packing her bags and moving again. She was starting a business and making Solomons her permanent home. Plus, the last time she gave up everything for a man, their love story had a sour ending.

# CHAPTER 16

*M*ackenzie strolled along the dock at Solomons Beach with her hands tucked in her pockets. It felt surreal walking alongside Alex, a man she'd never envisioned seeing again. Clearly, he felt the same, because he'd barely spoken a word since agreeing to meet with her. The weather for the day was fitting for her mood, a heavy overcast that lingered without a trace of sunlight in sight. All she could seem to think about was Stephanie and whether she was making the right decision by being there.

"Thank you for responding to my text message," she said, starting the conversation.

"No. Thank you. I should've been out of town by now, but the bus with all our equipment broke down, extending my stay just a little while longer."

"Mmm," she replied. "Seems kind of odd that you would follow your band around in a corvette. Do you normally travel separate from the group?"

"Oh, the corvette. That was just a fun rental for a couple of days. When we're on the road, we normally stick together." He smiled.

She nodded. "I see."

"Listen, Mack."

"It's Mackenzie." She corrected him.

"Sorry. Mackenzie. I realize this was probably difficult for you. But, I really do appreciate you meeting with me. I think you'll soon come to see just how much this will benefit Stephanie. A little girl ought to have a relationship with her father."

"While I don't disagree with that statement, I haven't decided yet. My mother raised me not to be so quick to allow strangers into your life."

She noticed Alex speaking, then catching himself, before proceeding cautiously.

"Fair enough. Although I'd hardly consider myself to be a complete stranger. We were married at some point. We knew each other very well."

Mackenzie stopped to make brief eye contact. "You don't want to go down that rabbit hole with me. As of today, you are a stranger to me. I know nothing about your lifestyle and whether it's safe to even introduce the idea of your name to my daughter. So, the better thing to do is to talk to me. Tell me what's been going on in your life since we last saw you."

She pressed forward, realizing she'd left him standing there dumbfounded, but she didn't care. If this was something he really wanted, she knew he'd catch up.

"Okay, uh, where do I begin? Let's see. I tried reaching out to you about six months after we started traveling. By then, we were doing a few shows abroad, living out of motels, barely getting by, but I called. Unfortunately, you disconnected the line."

She nodded.

"Yeah, that's what happens when you can no longer afford to pay the rent on your own. I had to pack up and find a realistic place to live in proximity to work and Stephanie's daycare. It was quite a nightmare for a while there. But, how does the saying go? What doesn't kill you strengthens you? Ha." She chuckled sarcastically.

Mackenzie found herself keeping a faster pace the more he shared his side of the story.

"Eventually, I tried to send you money. I even reached out to your family out west to ask them if they could help get the message across, but all I received was one dial tone after the other. They refused to speak to me."

"That would be my fault. Once I realized you were deciding to choose your career over us, I figured, why bother? I asked them not to take your calls and not to relay any messages."

He stopped. "How could you?"

She assumed her blood pressure had to be abnormally high. Her body felt overheated on a day where the temps barely reached seventy degrees. If it was her pressure, then it was definitely the outrageous comments coming out of his mouth that were pushing all the buttons and sounding all the internal alarms.

"You... abandoned... us. Therefore, giving me permission to do what I thought was best for me and Stephanie. It shouldn't come as a shock to you that I would move mountains to protect my baby girl. I would've done the same had you —" She stopped, drawing in a deep breath, then continued. "I'm sorry. I didn't come here to fight. I just need to know, before I decide to tell Stephanie about you, that you will not disappoint her. I need to know that you're serious, and that whatever you say you're going to do, you will stand by your word."

"I promise, I will."

This time she slowed down to regulate her heartbeat.

"Mmm. Why don't you continue telling me what life is like on the road?"

He began strolling alongside her again. "It is what you make it, I guess. We're no longer in motels anymore, but living in and out of hotels isn't exactly a desirable lifestyle either. It can feel lonely. The guys have their family members to go home and visit. Me... well, I pay up to maintain a healthy diet, hit the gym a few times a week, and perform at concerts so we can pay the bills. It's a job like anything else. The only difference is I travel."

"Hmm. Do you have a bunch of women and groupies following you around?"

Again, he seemed taken aback, but she noticed he was at least willing to go along with whatever she asked of him. Internally, she struggled with his ability to give everything up and walk away. After all the sacrifices she made. She didn't understand it, and she knew she probably never would.

"No. So far, I've still managed to keep a relatively low profile in big cities like the one near National Harbor. Folks around here would probably have to look me up first." He smiled, revealing the same dimples that captured her heart many years ago.

"What about you? Are you settled down with the guy who was with Stephanie the other day?" he asked.

"We're in a relationship."

"Is he good to you?" He continued.

"He's wonderful to both myself and Stephanie. He plays an active role in her life, and she loves him for it."

"Right."

They approached the end of the boardwalk where Mackenzie looked around before locking eyes with him.

"Bottom line, Alex, I don't think it's a good idea to start

with an in-person visit. When she's ready, you should call and talk over the phone first, allowing her to decide the pace and follow her lead. God knows I can't even explain where you've been all these years, but I guess I'll figure something out."

He approached her gingerly, appearing almost afraid to say or do the wrong thing.

"Might I suggest you don't have to explain the details to her? You shouldn't have to bear the entire burden on your own. I will be honest, communicating the best way I know how to a six-year-old that I made some wrong choices. Please, Mackenzie. I will be gentle, not pushing beyond what she can handle."

Mackenzie broke down, giving in, ultimately hoping she was doing the right thing.

~

Mackenzie refilled Stephanie's glass of milk, encouraging her to finish the last few carrots on her plate.

"Do I have to?" she asked.

It was their nightly routine as of late. No matter how many ways she dressed up her vegetables, broccoli in cheese, carrots with a light butter sauce, they were Stephanie's least favorite thing to eat.

"Young lady, if you can leave room for dessert, then you can eat your vegetables." She explained.

"Okay." She hadn't been a troublesome child, and in some ways, Mack couldn't blame her. She inherited her disdain for vegetables from her mother. Mack hated eating her veggies as a kid, no matter how much her grandmother tried to sweeten up her peas. But it was really the only thing Stephanie subtly resisted. Other than that, she was an angel.

"How was school today, love?"

"Good. A new girl started today. Her name is Toby. She

seems pretty nice." Stephanie revealed, scraping the last carrot off her plate and taking several gulps of her milk.

"That's great. I'm sure you wouldn't mind showing her the ropes. I'll bet your teacher could always use a helper to show the new students around."

"I'll try, but this other girl, Mary Ann, already invited her to be friends. And Mary Ann is not one of the nice girls. But that's okay. Toby will learn soon enough."

"Oh." Mack giggled, admiring her mature sense of humor.

"As long as you continue to lead by example, honey. That's what matters most. How's everything going with the kids who were bothering you at school?" Mack hated being that mom to press her child with several questions at the end of the day. She didn't want it to feel like she was being interviewed, but at this stage, she didn't know any other way. It seemed like the older she'd become, the less she talked.

"They're not bothering me anymore. Miss Cunningham said she'd give them lunch detention if it happened again."

Mack cocked her head toward Steph. "Now, that's my kind of teacher." She laughed.

Stephanie agreed, eagerly removing herself from the table to grab an ice cream cone.

"I just placed a new tub of strawberry in the freezer. Grab the scooper and make sure you don't go over two scoops, please."

"Okay, mom," she said.

Mackenzie cleared the table and rinsed off the last utensils, placing everything one by one in the dishwasher. She was nervous, with lingering thoughts of her conversation with Alex on her mind, but she tried not to let it show.

"Hey, love, I have to ask you something," she said.

Stephanie scraped her last scoop, patting it on the cone as only a pro could do.

"Yes, Mommy."

"It's been a while, sweetheart, but do you remember the last time we had a talk about your dad?" she asked.

"You mean when the girls at school were teasing me?"

Sweat escaped from Mack's pores. Finding the right words and trying to be ever so careful with her approach was tugging on her nervous system.

"No, honey. I'm talking about the last time you wanted to know more about your dad. We haven't talked about him in a while."

"Oh. I guess I don't think about it that much. Except for the time the girls were bothering me at school. It's probably because I have Brody now." She smiled, with a remnant of strawberry ice cream smeared across her face.

"Do you think you will marry Brody someday?" Stephanie smiled.

"Would you like me to?"

She took another lick from her ice cream cone. "Mm hmm. I like him a lot, Mommy."

"That's good to know. I think Brody would make a great addition to our family someday. But, in the meantime, what if I told you that your real dad would like to speak with you? Would you like that idea?"

Stephanie's eyes widened.

"I recently learned that your dad is still traveling with his band. But, he's feeling sad about missing the opportunity to see you grow up. He'd like to call you if that's something you think you would like," she said, as gingerly and carefully as she knew how. Mack prayed silently, waiting for her response.

"What about Brody? If I talk to my real dad, does this mean we can't be friends with Brody anymore?" Stephanie's face drooped, along with her ice cream that began melting down her fingers.

"No, love, of course not. Brody isn't going anywhere. He loves us. But, I'll bet when he finds out that you talked to your real dad, he'll be so happy for you. And, just so you know, there's no pressure to rush things. You get to be the one who decides when you talk, or if you talk at all. It's all up to you."

Looking up with her crystal blue eyes, she asked, "What do you want me to do, Mommy?"

On the inside, Mackenzie's heart tore into tiny little pieces. If only she could be granted one wish, it would be that this would all go away.

"I want you to follow your heart, love. You don't have to give me an answer now. Think about it and get back to me when you are ready."

# CHAPTER 17

*a*gnes revved up the motor to one of the jet skis, ensuring it was in good working condition. Brody was scheduled to stop by later, picking it up to use as a rental over at Lighthouse Tours. She'd spent the morning pulling the keys to a couple of boats that were scheduled to be picked up, and she had already gone over the morning checklist with Ben, the new employee. The only thing left to do was to somehow distract herself from missing Grant on such a quiet and dismal morning.

"Ben, thanks for your help with getting the boats ready. With your strength and my organizational skills, I think we make a great team," she said.

"I'd certainly have to agree. I'm thankful to Mike, Clara, and you for giving me the opportunity."

She innocently waved her finger. "Oh, no. You can't thank me. I'm a member of the family, yes, but I'm hardly in charge. The only thing I'm the boss of is that baby parked right over there," she said, pointing toward her truck.

"When will she be opened for business?" he asked.

"June first. Coming to a location near you. I can't wait."

"That's awesome. But may I ask, why wait until June? You have the entire month of May ahead of you."

Agnes' eyes fell slightly. "It's the anniversary of the day Clara and I lost our parents. I'm doing it sort of as a dedication to them. Plus, I think it's a great day to kick off the summer festivities, even though summer doesn't technically begin until later in the month."

Ben turned over the motor to another one of the jet skis, gave it the once over, and then cut it off.

"It sounds like you have a lot to be excited about. What I can't understand is why you have such a long face. You've had one for the last several days. Is everything okay?"

Kicking at a pile of rocks proved pointless, but that's exactly what Agnes found herself doing since she didn't know how to respond.

"Let me guess. It's your guy friend, isn't it? You two having trouble in paradise?" He chuckled.

"No. Well, yes. Maybe. To tell you the truth, I really don't know what to call it."

She observed his lingering smile while he fiddled around with the equipment. Ben looked to be about the same age as Agnes, wearing a short buzz cut from his military days, and dog tags, which he wore every day. They weren't the real ones, he explained, but they were bought as a gift in memory of his grandfather, who'd lost his life at war.

"Okay. Well, I'm no expert or anything, but I am a man. So, if you ever need any advice from a guy's perspective, I'd be happy to help. The offer stands only if you feel comfortable, of course," he said.

"Nah, I'm good. I wouldn't want to bore you with my pathetic life."

He looked at her.

"You sure? Somehow, I doubt your life is pathetic. Plus, it might be a great way to pass the time."

She thought about it. Perhaps all she needed was a stroll down to the water alone to clear her mind. Even though the thought of getting advice from a male's perspective did sound enticing.

Ben continued. "How about this? Next time he calls, tell him how much you miss him. I'm sure that will resolve whatever the problem is," he said.

She burst into laughter, shaking her head at the idea. If that's all she needed to do, then it would already be a done deal. Grant wouldn't be in Tennessee with his family. He'd instead be right there by her side.

"I already did. That didn't get me very far." She admitted.

"Oh, well, in that case, he's not the right guy for you. That was easy. Problem solved."

That brought her head up, causing her to relinquish an eye roll or two.

"It's not as easy as you make it sound. Grant really is a nice guy. He just travels for his job, so it's a little more complicated than saying I miss you and expecting everything to magically come together like a fairytale," she said, flailing her hands in the air in a whimsical kind of way.

Ben chuckled.

"See, that's the problem with women. You're always making excuses for deadbeat men, selling yourselves short in the interim. If he's all that you say he is, he needs to be right here on Solomons Island, doing everything he can to hold on to you."

She paused, considering his feedback. "I didn't exactly make things easy when he was here. It's not an excuse. It's just the God's honest truth. I actually tried to avoid him, except I wasn't very good at it in the end."

Ben looked up, holding a push broom in his hand. "Interesting. Well, I guess I was wrong. Maybe your life is pretty pathetic, after all. Perhaps you need to try out one of those dating apps instead. Maybe you'll have better luck that way." He laughed, returning to his chores.

"Ha... ha... ha... very funny. Thanks for the rotten advice. You definitely need to stick to your day job." She teased. "I think next time I'll bite my tongue. At this rate, I'd be better off lying on a couch in a therapist's office," Agnes said, making a beeline for her quiet spot toward the back of the property.

"I'll be back in ten," she yelled, disappearing toward the boat slips.

Almost a week later, Mackenzie paced frantically around the living room with Brody, trying his best to calm her down. She joined Stephanie on the phone call with her dad for the first few minutes, then exited the room, allowing them time to speak alone. Her bangs flopped into the air as she exhaled, trying to relieve the stress. It wasn't working. Any minute now, she had a plan to burst back in the door, putting a time restriction on their conversation.

"Maybe I should put my ear up to the door to make sure she's okay."

"Mackenzie, the door is cracked open and from what I can tell, she sounds happy," Brody said.

"Mm hmm. I think five or ten minutes, tops, for the first conversation is sufficient. I mean, good grief, how much can he expect out of a six-year-old during their first telephone call?"

The sound of laughter came out of Stephanie's room, throwing Mack off guard.

"I guess he figured out something to help them make a

connection. She sounds fine, Mack. The question is, how are you doing?" Brody asked, hugging her close.

"Do you want the truth?"

"Always," he replied.

"I'm nervous. What if Stephanie will be upset with me for not trying to find him? What if she asks me to visit with him or, even worse, wants to live with him someday? I don't think I can handle it, Brody."

"Shh. Mackenzie, you're torturing yourself, imagining the worst case scenario. What if this turns out to be the best decision you ever made for her? You would always wonder if you hadn't done what you did today."

"Yes, but what if I went about this the wrong way? Maybe I should've waited longer before allowing him to speak to her."

Surprise rose in Mackenzie as she watched her daughter skip out of the room, passing her the cell phone. "Here, Mom, he wants to talk to you."

She slowly raised the phone to her ear. "Hello."

"Mackenzie, thank you so much for doing this. It means the world to me. I explained to Stephanie that I'm on the road, but she can call and talk to me whenever she wants to. I want you to know that I don't plan on forcing the relationship. I'm going to take you up on your suggestion, allowing Stephanie to lead at a pace that makes her feel comfortable. I didn't even say anything about my gig at the Harbor. I figure it would be best to leave that up to you."

Mack watched as Stephanie twirled her pink tutu around the living room. She noticed Brody's brown eyes were filled with empathy. She exhaled, giving herself permission to put her own mind at ease.

"I appreciate it. I just ask that you remember our agreement to uphold your promises to her. The last thing she needs is a broken heart."

She listened to him for another minute, then hit the red button, ending the call after saying their goodbyes. As expected, Stephanie bombarded her with a ton of questions. But, mostly, she was impressed that her father was a rock star. Whether Stephanie understood the full impact, their reconnection would have remained unknown. But, at least for now, and for the first time, she heard the voice of her dad.

"Baby, come here. Tell me... how did you feel about your telephone call?" Mackenzie asked.

Brody sat on a bar stool, giving them time together.

"He said he's been thinking about me. And, wondering what it would be like to talk to me someday."

"Wow, lovey. How does that make you feel?" Mackenzie asked.

"Sad and happy at the same time. I told him I wish he knew me since I was a baby. If he did, then he would know that I'm pretty funny and very good at gymnastics."

A smile emerged from Mackenzie. "Ha, that's so true."

"I also told him I know what he looks like because you saved a lot of pictures of him." Stephanie confessed.

Mack glanced over at Brody, who quietly bowed his head.

"That's also true. Mommy always thought it was important that you have special pictures to call your own."

"Hey, Mom."

"Yes, love."

"Do you think I could call dad again some time? He said it was okay if you approved," she asked.

"Of course, you can. But, for now, if you're going to make it to your friend's birthday party on time, then you need to get in your room and change."

"Yay, I love birthday parties."

Stephanie skipped to her room, leaving as lighthearted as only a child could do.

"Isn't that something?" Mackenzie nodded, partially talking to herself and then Brody.

"I spent all these years in denial, thinking we'd never see him again. Then poof, just like that, he's back in our lives, inflicting so many emotions, I don't know which way is up or down," she said.

Brody motioned for her to come closer to him.

"I don't know what it's like to be in your shoes right now, so I will not pretend to have the right advice. But, I'll tell you this. You are a resilient woman. There's not one struggle that's come your way that I haven't seen you bounce back from. You'll make it through this as well."

She buried her nose in his collar. "Thank you, Brody. You always know the right thing to say. I hope you know this doesn't change the way I feel about you one bit. The only ties I have to Alex is our daughter. But this doesn't change my love for you."

"Well, I'm so glad to hear it, because Lord knows I'm in love with you."

# CHAPTER 18

"So, it's May thirty-first and tomorrow is the big day. Are you feeling nervous?" Clara asked. Agnes hoisted herself off the back of the truck, parked in her sister's driveway, smiling and admiring its beauty. "I suppose I should be, but the only thing I feel is excitement, really. I'm ready to get the show on the road. This has been a dream of mine for a long time. Now seeing it finally come to fruition means a lot," she said.

Clara unloaded the last plastic bag filled with utensils in the back of Agnes' truck. "I think I understand exactly what you mean. I've witnessed a few of my dreams become a reality, and well, the feeling is nothing short of amazing," she said, glancing at her wedding rings.

Agnes shook her head. "Now, that's an accomplishment I've yet to check off my list. Have you gotten used to people referring to you as Mrs. Sanders yet?"

"Yes and no. I mean, I love the sound of my new name, but I've been Clara Covington my whole life. I think it's going to take some getting used to. But overall marrying Mike has been the best thing that's ever happened to me. That and of course, having my little sister back in my life."

Agnes chuckled. "Why thank you. I hope you know the feeling is mutual."

Holly circled around them, sniffing around for undetected treats.

"Clara, when I look at how things came together in your life, I can't help but think of how proud mom and dad would be. You found an amazing man to spend your life with, you work hard, and technically you don't even have to. Plus, you're admired by so many here."

"I disagree with the part about working hard. Hard work is a part of my DNA. It keeps your mind sharp. Isn't that what dad used to say?" Clara snarled, playfully.

"Yes, but you get where I'm going with this. You and Mike built a dream life together, and I can't see it going anywhere but up from here on out. Honestly, I want to be just like you and Mike when I grow up. Maybe I'll add a horse and buggy at my private ceremony, but everything else can be exactly the same, including the fabulous trip to Hawaii."

"Agnes, you'll have everything your heart desires and more. In due time it will happen. Trust me. I'm just happy to hear you admit that you're open to the idea of getting married. I guess the whole sabbatical was kind of lame after all?"

"Lame is an understatement. I miss Grant," Agnes said, holding her head down.

Clara drew her in for a side hug. "Cheer up. I know it's the last thing you want to hear right now, but even that situation will work itself out in due time. And, if it doesn't, then you'll make room in your heart for the person you're really meant to be with. Either way, mom and dad would be equally as proud of you, sis."

"Thank you." Agnes smiled.

"You know, what? In celebration of your big day tomorrow, I think we should raid the chocolate ice cream. Mike's working late at the office tonight. What do you say?" Clara nudged her.

"You know that's my favorite flavor. I'm all in."

On June first, Agnes slid open the window of her food truck, hanging her sign to announce she was open for business. With time to spare before the afternoon rush, she tied on her apron and set up a chart displaying all of her menu options. Against her original plans, she hired someone to help her run the cash register while she managed the cooking and the orders.

The meat ranged from mouth-watering barbecue chicken to spare ribs with several sauce options and sides to make anyone stop and inquire. Now, all she needed was a crowd. She figured the delicious aroma coming from her smoker would draw them in, but it was still left to be seen.

"Monahan, I can't thank you enough for saying yes to the job. I don't know what I was thinking. Between managing the grill and putting together the orders, I would've been running around like a chicken with my head cut off. One would think I would've realized it way before now," Agnes said.

"Are you kidding me? It thrilled me to hear your voice on the other end of the line when you called. We worked so well together at the Seafood Shack. For me, this was a no brainer. Plus, I could really use the extra change. The job I picked up after Lucille let us go is okay, but the hours don't compare. I always find myself watching my pennies, so trust me, this was a blessing for both of us."

Monica, affectionately known as Monahan to the old crew at the Seafood Shack, made sure the ice container was filled to the brim, the cups were stocked to full capacity, and simple items like straws and napkins were ready on hand.

"So, how have things been going with you since we last saw each other? I knew you were always busy sketching out plans for the truck, but boy oh boy, you should be proud of yourself, Agnes. You actually made your dream become a reality." She smiled, admiring the establishment.

"I know, it's kind of crazy. For a while I parked this baby at my brother-in-law's business, and I quietly questioned if I could really do it. Now that the sign is up, I just need to bring the dollars in, proving to myself this whole thing wasn't done in vain," Agnes said, flopping her hand at her side.

"Don't worry. We're pros. Well, to be clear, you're the pro with the culinary skills, but I have your back in the customer service department," Monahan replied, giving Agnes a high five.

"Oh my gosh, here's my first customer." Agnes positioned herself to lean out of the window, greeting her first customer with a huge smile. "Welcome to The BBQ Hut, how may I help you?" she nervously blurted out, darn near scaring the woman with her high-pitched voice.

Thankfully, she was easily distracted by the large menu filled with an array of options.

"Um, I think I'll have the Rockin Ribs, mild, with a side of coleslaw, please. If you could put a cup of extra sauce on the side, that would be great."

Agnes immediately grabbed a to-go container. "Sure, can I get you anything to drink with your order?"

"No, thank you."

"Alrighty. One Rockin Ribs order, coming right up."

The first order would be a breeze, as thankfully, she'd cooked a few slabs ahead of time. She could put the hot order together quickly, adding a fresh batch of coleslaw, and her signature sauce. Once complete, she bagged everything up and took the woman's credit card to complete the transaction.

"Thank you for stopping by. Enjoy!" Agnes again smiled enthusiastically while Monica watched her.

"Look at you, Agnes. You're a natural. I had no idea. Do you mind if I have a sample of your sauce during my break?"

Agnes grabbed a spoon, scooping up a sample into one of her cups. "Brilliant idea. How about you sample it now? It's the only way you can truly sell the product. Try it with a piece of chicken or a rib. The more familiar you are with the unique flavors, the more you can help talk it up."

She made a sampler plate for Monica, including a few meat options, potato salad, the coleslaw, and a few fries as an added bonus.

"Okay, I'll take over the front window while you stay back here and give this plate a try. Don't hold back. I want your honest opinion," Agnes said.

After checking to see that no one was coming, she watched Monahan sink her teeth in, closing her eyes after the very first bite. "Shut... the front door!" She let the words ease out in between bites.

"What?"

"Girl, you're really talented. You've been holding out on me," Monahan replied, stuffing her face with potato salad. "This is Solomons Island's best kept secret. You keep cooking like this, you'll be opening up a full-blown restaurant in no time."

Agnes shook her head, disagreeing with her last statement. "Nope. No brick and mortars for me. The whole beauty in starting a food truck is that it allows me to be creative, flexible, and I don't have to deal with the overhead. If the truck doesn't work out, then I'll have my warehouse position to fall back on. That's as far as the vision goes for now," she said.

"All right. If you say so. In the meantime, this is really good. I mean, really, really good."

A man's voice interrupted their conversation. "I'd like to try some, please."

Agnes jumped, easily startled at the sound of his voice being so close.

"Grant," she whispered, softly. The feeling of instant heat rising through the upper portion of her body was enough to make her conscious.

"What are you doing here?"

He looked around at her sign and pretended to look for other customers in line before smiling at her. "Rumor has it that today is opening day for The BBQ Hut. I was grabbing a cup of coffee, hoping to run into this beautiful woman I know, when a man by the name of Harvey told me where you were located. I thought I'd be one of the first few to sample the menu, if that's okay."

"Oh, sure. What would you like to try?" she asked.

He pointed over toward the menu. "I'll take one of each."

"But you just pointed to the entire menu. Surely, you don't want everything."

Monahan moved over to the window beside her, mumbling in a low voice. "Who is that fine specimen of a man?"

Agnes held her hand below the window, trying feverishly to swat at her.

"Are you two an item?" Monahan continued.

Grant chuckled. "I wish we were. That's been my goal for a while now. But, this lady, here... well, let's just say she's one tough cookie. It's okay, though. I'm not one to easily give up. At least not without putting my best effort forward," he said.

A smile appeared across Agnes' face with the sweetest

sound of laughter. "I think you've put in your fair share of effort."

"Oh no, you haven't seen anything yet. You see, I just spent the last two weeks boxing up all my things. I kissed my folks goodbye, told them I'd visit again soon, and now—" He looked at his watch.

"Now, I'm expecting a moving truck to show up at the beach house in about an hour. Figured I'd stop by here and purchase a few items on the menu to share with the guys and have some extra for later."

Agnes could feel her heart thumping in tandem with the butterflies fluttering in her stomach. Everything felt like it was pulsating out of control. The magnetic heat they shared was enough to make Monahan back away, giving them their privacy.

"You left Tennessee?" she asked.

"Tennessee, Colorado, New York, San Francisco, and every other state that I have marked on my map. I left it all to be here in Solomons... with you. I just signed on the dotted line and closed on the house today."

She gripped the counter, hoping and praying her legs wouldn't give in.

"Grant, I —"

"Please, Agnes. Join me tonight after you get off. I'll be up at the house unpacking boxes. Maybe we could take a stroll down by the water and talk things over," he said, leaning in closer. "These last couple of months of talking and texting aren't enough anymore. We belong together. And, unless you disagree with me, please. Meet me tonight at the beach house."

As a customer approached to get in line, she nodded. "I'll stop by tonight."

Monahan approached the window with multiple bags, placing them on the front counter. "Here you go, sir. One of everything on the menu, just as you ordered. Plus extra sauce. The soft drink is on the house. Oh, and if you leave a nice tip in the jar, I'll make sure she arrives at your place nice and early," she said, winking at Mack.

Agnes and Grant laughed together, enjoying every bit of Monahan's sense of humor.

He then reached into his crossbody satchel and pulled out something to hand to Agnes. "I want to give this to you before I forget." It was his book. The first copy, signed and delivered as promised.

Agnes Covington gazed around, noticing boxes stacked everywhere. She'd let herself in as he'd instructed in a text, but no longer recognized the place with its bland walls. The maps that told a story of his travels were missing, along with his art and all evidence of his writing.

"Grant, I'm here." She called out, strolling toward the kitchen. On the counters was evidence of his visit to her food truck earlier in the day.

"Lucky me. Not only are you here, but you look gorgeous as always," he said, startling her with his low voice from behind. He approached with two glasses in hand. "By some sort of miracle, I found two wine glasses. Would you like to join me out back? I'd set up a place for us indoors but listening to the sound of the water is way more appealing." He offered.

"Sure, after you."

Outside, he set up a small table with a glass of wine and two recycled containers with a fork and knife resting on the top. She recognized the containers and laughed.

"Now, this is a first. I've been on dates before, but none that involved me eating my own food."

Grant passed her a couple of napkins. "Ha, I thought this might be original," he said, gazing into her eyes. "I was out this afternoon when I came across a new food truck with an aroma that smelled so delicious, I couldn't help but stop by. The owner's assistant was kind enough to make sure I sampled everything." He teased.

"I think it was the other way around. You asked for everything on the menu, making yourself my biggest customer of the day."

Grant slid his hand over hers, generating the same electricity she'd experienced earlier. "I'll gladly be your biggest customer, but more importantly, I'm your biggest fan. It felt good being here for your big day. I'm hoping to be around for other important events in your life, just like it." He confessed.

Agnes' eyes fell slightly, noticing that he wasn't letting go of her hand, and she liked it.

"My sister would have to argue with you about being my biggest fan. She arrived shortly after you left, helping to drum up a crowd. Clara is a natural when it comes to marketing," she responded.

"Agnes."

"Yes?"

"There's plenty here to eat in just a few minutes, but that's not why I called you here tonight. If I have to hold off any longer from telling you how I really feel, I think I'll lose my mind," he said.

"Nobody wants that," she replied.

"Good. First, let me say that I love you. Before I left, you told me you didn't think a long-distance relationship would work. So, to honor your wishes, I played by the rules, continuing on with my life with plans to travel. The only problem is I can't do this anymore. I can't pack my bags on a whim, traveling carefree the way I used to, and I know that my feelings have changed because of you."

"Grant —"

"No, let me finish," he said, turning to hold both of her hands. "I realize I took a big chance buying a property and moving all the way back to Solomons Island. I knew there would always be a risk, that you could still refuse to be with me. But, I don't care. It's a risk I'm willing to take."

Grant chuckled, leaning back in his chair. She observed him lost in his own thoughts, grappling with the best way to express his feelings.

"It's almost crazy to think that I'd fall so deep. You and I spent more time at odds in the beginning than not," he said, causing them both to laugh.

He continued. "But none of that matters. I want to spend my days creating memories right here on Solomons Island with you. And I know it sounds crazy, but I really hope you feel the same way too."

An electrifying surge ran through her core, leaving her speechless.

"Agnes, help me out here. I don't know whether I'm saying all the right things or if I'm drowning without a running chance." He pleaded.

She slid her hand over the side of his cheek, bringing her lips within inches of his. "Well, since I'm allowed to talk now, my heart tells me you're doing a great job. I particularly like the part about you loving me because I love you too. And I also like the part about creating memories with you."

"Are you serious?" he asked.

"No. Absolutely not. I'm playing a ridiculous prank on you and any moment now, in the spirit of being difficult, I'm about to walk right out the front —" Grant placed his finger gently over her lips, hushing the sound of her silly babbling.

"Kiss me." She mumbled underneath his finger.

He leaned in, gliding his lips in between hers, only after several strokes coming up briefly to say, "You don't have to ask me twice."

*Continue following the Solomons Island saga in book six, Beachfront Secrets!*

# NEW TROPICAL BREEZE SERIES!

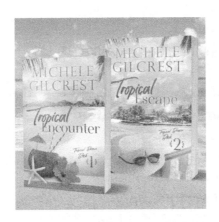

***Can she find love when she's healing from heartache?***

After a painful end to a long engagement, all Meg wants out of life is a fresh start.

She can't think of a better way to begin than by advancing her career in the hotel industry. When an opportunity comes along to accept a position at a five-star resort, she secures a beach house, packs her bags, and heads to the Bahamas.

But her oasis has been sold in an auction and the new owner and heartthrob, Parker Wilson, has no intention of holding onto a contract.

She'll have nowhere to stay, nowhere to heal, nowhere to grow if she gives in to his flippant attitude about her future.

When Meg digs her heels in and refuses to leave, will this drive them further into the arena of enemies? Or will they find common ground and potentially become lovers?

Tropical Encounter is a clean beach read with a splash of romance that's sure to give you all the feels.

**Pull up your favorite beach chair and watch as Meg and Parker's story unfolds!**

*Tropical Breeze Series:*
> *Tropical Encounter: Book 1*
> *Tropical Escape: Book 2*
> *Tropical Moonlight: Book 3*
> *Tropical Summers: Book 4*
> *Tropical Brides: Book 5*

# SOLOMONS ISLAND SERIES

**She's single, out of a job, and has a week to decide what to do with her life.**

**He lost his fiancé to a fatal accident while serving in the coast guard.**

**Will a chance encounter lead Clara and Mike to find love?**

*Clara's boss, Joan Russell, was a wealthy owner of a beachfront mansion, who recently passed away. Joan's estranged family members have stepped in, eager to collect their inheritance and dismiss Clara of her duties.*

*With the clock winding down, will Clara find a job and make a new life for herself on Solomons Island? Will a chance encounter with Mike lead her to meet the man of her dreams? Or will Clara have to do the unthinkable and return home to a family who barely cares for her existence?*

**This women's divorce fiction book will definitely leave you wanting more! If you love women's fiction and clean romance, this series is for you. Embark on a journey of new beginnings and pick up your copy today!**

**<u>Solomons Island Series:</u>**

**Beachfront Inheritance: Book 1**

**Beachfront Promises: Book 2**

**Beachfront Embrace: Book 3**

**Beachfront Christmas: Book 4**

**Beachfront Memories: Book 5**

**Beachfront Secrets: Book 6**

# PELICAN BEACH SERIES

**She's recently divorced. He's a widower. Will a chance encounter lead to true love?**

If you like sweet romance about second chances then you'll love The Inn At Pelican Beach!

At the Inn, life is filled with the unexpected. Payton is left to pick up the pieces after her divorce is finalized. Seeking a fresh start, she returns to her home town in Pelican Beach.

Determined to move on with her life, she finds herself

caught up in the family business at The Inn. It may not be her passion, but anything is better than what her broken marriage had to offer. Payton doesn't wallow in her sorrows long before her opportunity at a second chance shows up. Is there room in her heart to love again? She'll soon find out!

In this first book of the Pelican Beach series, passion, renewed strength, and even a little sibling rivalry are just a few of the emotions that come to mind.

Visit The Inn and walk hand in hand with Payton as she heals and seeks to restore true love.

**Get your copy of this clean romantic beach read today!**

**Pelican Beach Series:**
   **The Inn at Pelican Beach: Book 1**
   **Sunsets at Pelican Beach: Book 2**
   **A Pelican Beach Affair: Book 3**
   **Christmas at Pelican Beach: Book 4**
   **Sunrise At Pelican Beach: Book 5**

Made in the USA
Middletown, DE
17 November 2023

42856871R00110